Shattering the Effects of Time

Finding the Fountain of Youth

By

C. A. King

Cover Design: Just Write Creations

Editor: J.D. Cunegan

This book is dedicated to those who crave the Nano Eggs.

Seek and receive!

Otters shall inherit the World.

Look for other books by C.A. King, including:

The Portal Prophecies:

Book I - A Keeper's Destiny

Book II - A Halloween's Curse

Book III - Frost Bitten

Book IV - Sleeping Sands

Book V - Deadly Perceptions
Book VI - Finding Balance

Tomoiya's Story:

Book I: Escape to Darkness
Book II: Collecting Tears

Surviving the Sins:

Book I: Answering the Call
Book II: Pride

When Leaves Fall: A Different Point of View Story

Peach Coloured Daisies: A Cursed by the Gods Story

Flower Shields: A Four Horsemen Novel

Cover Design: **Just Write Creations**

First Printing: September 2017
2nd Edition: November 2017

ISBN: 978-1-988301-29-7

Kings Toe Publishing
kingstoepublishing@gmail.com
Burlington, Ontario. Canada

Prologue

Balance - the simple mention of the word has been known to invoke an image of a person walking on a tightrope, high above the ground, with no net. Each footstep would have to have been placed carefully - outstretched arms teetering up and down - back and forth. Falling was never an option. In a performance, the rope was a short distance - in life, it never ended. It was that balance that made existence possible. To fail and tumble on either side could have been devastating. One trembling footstep steadied was the reason the next began to wobble. Cause and effect was a concept that should have been considered carefully by everyone. Unfortunately, it rarely was.

The Portal Prophecies may have saved the realms from Cornelius and Cornost, but by doing so, they opened doors to new problems. One could have said the metaphoric rope was shaken - its threads quivering. As a result, traversing it without tumbling became harder than it ever was before.

Change was inevitable in the Universe. A plant that sprouted from the ground as a tiny shoot grew into a blooming flower and then withered away to seed. That very action brought new sprouts to life in the future. Some grew in the same spot, while others were whisked away by the wind to bring new scenery to lands previously untouched by their kind.

So, too, William's camp changed. The guardians were free to choose their own paths. Some returned to their home land to help rebuild and others remained to establish new futures - choosing different keepers or to have none. The recently-formed symbiotic relationships between two life forces weren't created without their share of problems. Something was lacking - perhaps the synergy, or trust that had been taken for granted in the past.

The camp itself split in several different directions. One group headed home with the guardians to rebuild their world for future generations. Those who remained in the camp swore oaths to continue to defend the portals. Jade and Malarchy stayed in Pewterclaw to forge a life in the political scene of the magical cities located in the main world. Their saga was already unfolding with the possibility of another battle looming over their heads.

For Jessie, Dezi, and Pete, a new journey was just beginning. The aftermath of battles already fought left creatures, thought dormant, stirring and one young girl fighting for her life.

Victoria, a healer merely ten cycles old, mimicked what she had once witnessed Willow do, infusing her magic with her own life essence in order to save the lives of those she cared about most. Without that sacrifice, the casualty list in the camp would have skyrocketed and only a handful of individuals would have survived Lara's attack, if any at all.

There was, however, a price for the magic that she used. Victoria's ability wasn't advanced enough to handle the strain. In the end, she aged rapidly beyond her years, leaving her lying in stasis - a child trapped in an aged woman's frail body.

Nick was able to use his abilities to slow the effect of time around her, but the clock was still ticking - inevitably, one day time would run out.

While there was no known magic that could reverse the effects of aging, there were rumours of artifacts throughout the main world that possibly could. Every terunji tale had some truth to it. The young healer's life depended on at least one of those legends being based on fact rather than fiction. The Fountain of Youth, as elusive as it was, could have held the answer.

Victoria's brothers, Jessie, Dezi and Pete, set out to find a cure for their sister's ailment before time ran out completely. Armed only with a business card, a few maps, tales in a language unknown and a strange box, they headed off to find an underwater race of Mermaids thought to hold the knowledge of the location of the Fountain of Youth. Together with a less-than-honest Professor Finkle and a self-proclaimed Water Goddess, Pandora, the quest began...

Opening Thoughts

Some families passed things between generations. A wedding dress; jewelry; traditions; culture; recipes; and knowledge were only a few examples. These heirlooms were protected, cherished, and relished as a special bond shared between parent and child in an unbreakable cycle. They became a celebrated part of the growing identities of the young.

There were others, however, who were born into a life in which they were faced with sworn duties handed on by birthright - these responsibilities defined who they became. While not everyone wanted the tasks set before them, all complied. Occasionally, the Universe had other plans in store for an individual - one that combined the life they were born to live and the unknown that waited patiently in the future.

Chapter One

Time - an unusual thing. For some, it was always impossible to manage and easy to lose track of. With a temperament of its own, few have ever been able judge it. It couldn't be outrun, but definitely could run out. If there was one thing Nadine knew for certain about time, it was that it slowed to a crawl when she was falling. Those few seconds before impact were life's way of punishing the clumsy - forcing them to see the pain that was coming and know there was nothing that could be done to stop it.

Nadine pushed herself to a sitting position. Instinctively, she rubbed the side of her head - a lump was already forming. Soccer balls were hard, especially when they made contact with a person's temple. The force of Danny's kick had sent it hurtling towards her from the side faster than she could move. The result was an up-close and personal view of the grass - something she'd already seen more than her fair share of.

She brushed off her uniform as best she could. There were stains that stood out against the white material. Those were the worst. Some people could get away with grass and dirt smudges on their clothes and, in some cases, skin - it almost looked natural for them. Nadine, however, always felt her darker skin tone made any spot more noticeable. Even spaghetti was the enemy. She'd sworn it off for fear of splatter.

Examining the mess, she muttered a few choice words under her breath about the uniforms not being all black, or at least a dark navy blue. It seemed the obvious choice to keep appearances pristine, not to mention the money that could be saved on bleach. Complaining out loud was pointless. It would only draw further attention in her direction. If the Overseers hadn't changed the attire in centuries, they weren't about to do it now on her suggestion.

Still staggering to her feet, Nadine realized everyone was staring at her - a few girls giggling. She huffed out a puff of air, blowing a few ringlets gone wild off her face. There was no avoiding the teasing. In a way, she'd expected it. A simple look at the calendar was enough to know today wasn't going to go well. Sports day was the worst day of the year. She was no athlete and most of her peers were.

The coach motioned for her to move to a bench - a familiar place. She'd watch the rest of the day pass by from that very spot and was happy to have an excuse to do so. At least from there, she couldn't make a bigger fool of herself than she already had. She winced, her fingers running over the bump on her head. Luckily, there was no blood this time.

Danny flashed her a toothy smile and a wink. "You okay?" His blonde hair flipped back out of his face as if it had a mind of its own. Time was at work again - slowing down the motion just enough to watch every hair fall perfectly in place.

Nadine nodded her reply, temporarily losing her ability to speak. Sweaty, nervous hands found each other behind her back. Danny dripped with charisma, leaving most females and some males in the same boat as her. He knew it too, stringing them along like baubles in a handmade necklace - each wanting to be displayed front and centre. Only glamour could dazzle pizzazz. Each of his followers were almost as impressive in appearance and abilities as he was himself.

Soccer was only a warmup. There were far more difficult activities to come before the sun went down. Nadine cringed, thinking about the worst of them: obstacle courses; hand-to-hand combat; and sparring, already knowing she'd fail miserably at each and every one. No matter what she tried, her feet simply couldn't understand what her brain was saying. That meant an unusually large supply of bandages in her room and a first-name relationship with the resident nurse.

Merliance Academy wasn't a typical school. It was more of a training facility for those burdened with the task of protecting and aiding Mermaids. She could already hear her parents' words: *There are many positions that need to be filled, including intellectual ones.* That was the only area Nadine excelled at. She was smart - smarter than the average genius.

She'd given up fighting the inevitable. Upon graduation, the student body would be divided into teams based on their areas of expertise. Danny and his groupies would no doubt become field agents. Nadine, on the other hand, was destined for a basement office where the freshest air she'd breathe in would come from turning on a fan. A whimper escaped her throat. Didn't she deserve better?

"Head inside and have the medical staff check out that lump," the coach ordered before blowing a whistle. "Line it up!" he yelled to the team. "Danny, show these clowns how to do it!"

Nadine chuckled under her breath. That pretty much summed things up. There was the right way, the wrong way, and Danny's way. At any given time, two of those choices could randomly combine, becoming the same.

She headed off the field. There was no point arguing with the coach - that would only prolong the agony of boredom. Outside, in the midst of the physically superior, wasn't where she wanted to be anyways. Heat rushed to her ears, turning them red no doubt from the mal intent of a few stray comments about her lack of coordination. She shrugged it off, making her way inside. The squeaking of the rubber soles of her shoes on the floor echoed in the hallway now completely void of the usual day-to-day traffic. She muffled a chuckle. Empty was the perfect word to describe how she felt.

Her pace slowed to a crawl - a trophy box containing tributes to heroes of the past demanding her attention. Her fingers brushed against the smooth glass exterior, but her gaze didn't falter from the empty corridor. She knew every inch of the display, right down to the faces of her own great-grandparents front and centre. A sigh escaped on her breath. She wasn't anything like her great-grandmother - not an ounce of hero was to be found, yet everyone always searched for one. That look of disappointment when it couldn't be found was more painful than any words.

"Hey, champ."

Nadine's father had a way of sneaking up on her that sent goosebumps sprinting up and down her body. All Merliance members had at least one hidden talent. His happened to be stealth, although Nadine was sure there was more to it than being able to sneak up on his daughter.

"Hi, Dad," she replied, turning to face him and immediately wishing she hadn't. There was a flicker in his eyes that screamed disappointment - the very look she had hoped to avoid. It might have only had a split-second life, but it had been there and it was caused by her.

"Tough day?" he asked, forcing a half-smile. He pushed a stray curl from his daughter's face. It sprung right back out again, rebellious to the core.

Nadine turned her focus to the cabinet. "Yeah," she replied. "They look so happy. I wish I was more like her. Maybe if I had known her, things would be different."

"You can't change who you are," her father replied. "You need to find out about yourself and embrace it. Neither your mother nor myself would want you to live trying to be someone you aren't. Have a little faith - the world has a plan for you. One day, that plan will become clear."

"I wish that day would hurry up," Nadine answered, leaning her head against her father's shoulder. "Everyone expects me to do something great - to be like her. How can I live up to our namesake?"

"You aren't listening," her father whispered, kissing the top of her head. "You don't have to. In time, your path will come to you. Be patient."

Nadine nodded, offering the same forced half-smile back as she had previously received - a family trait. Advice was easy to give, but not as easy to live. There were certain expectations that came along with being a descendant of Viola Jones. She was, after all, the woman responsible for saving the world from the cries of the Mermaids.

According to the tales handed down through generations, Viola had been the one responsible for apprehending a band of would-be bandits who had managed to steal seven Mermaid eggs. Together with her husband, George, they set out to return the stolen property. The glass display cabinet was all there was to remember them by. There were no books or records. There weren't even any family pictures or mementos. If they hadn't been considered heroes, it would be hard to tell they ever existed. Ironically enough, their claim to fame was found in silence.

The wailing noises of a single crying Mermaid was thought to be powerful enough to move the earth. That fateful day, tremors were felt in all reaches of the realms. As fast as it started, it stopped. Tears were dried, allowing silence to return. Once again the Universe proved there are some things that need to remain hidden from the masses. Mermaids, their powers, and their way of life fell into that category. Merliance was a secret organization with renewed purpose and refreshed commitment from its members. That was the last time anyone saw her great-grandparents or a Mermaid.

Chapter Two

Jessie alternated glances between the white card in his hand and the sign hanging on the fence before them, though hanging was a rather relative term. It was actually rocking slightly, its only support coming from a lone surviving corner bolt. Even that was in rough shape. As a sign, it had only one job - now rust and dirt threatened to erase the very name it was meant to display. He glanced down at the strange business card one more time, trying to find some mistake, but finding none. If you took away the grime, the two matched. This was the place - the only problem was, it seemed abandoned.

Seagulls overhead squawked their displeasure of being disturbed. This was their feeding ground - rotting fish their favourite snack. From the smell, it was clear there was plenty of that nearby.

"It doesn't look like anyone has been here in years," Dezi complained.

Professor Finkle rolled his eyes. "Did you expect them to have a welcome mat or perhaps some tea with cookies?" He hugged a box tightly to his chest, making sure the picture of a Mermaid holding a large pearl on it was hidden from sight. If anyone was going to carry such a piece, it was him - especially since it was his life's work. That was something he wasn't about to let anyone forget.

"Well, no," Dezi answered. He brushed his sandy-coloured hair off his face. He'd left it a little too long between cuts and, more often than not, it got in the way. Not even that was going to help in this situation. "But look at this place. It's falling apart. The sign isn't even in good condition."

Professor Finkle sighed. Pulling a handkerchief out of his top pocket, he dabbed a few droplets of sweat from his brow. Once used, he stuffed it back in his jacket with little care for appearance. "It's a secret organization. It only makes sense they want you to think nothing is here. It wouldn't be very secret if they announced and showed themselves to the world, now would it?"

"He has a point," Jessie admitted.

"So what now?" Pete asked. "Do we barge in?" He took only one step forward before Finkle's hand grasped his shoulder, pulling him back.

"Slow down there," the Professor demanded. He pushed passed the boys and threw a stone at the fence. The brothers ducked, avoiding a shower of sparks falling down around them followed by a low-buzzing noise.

"It's an electric fence," Pete complained. "That could have killed us!"

"Yes," Finkle agreed, rolling his eyes. "You three aren't the brightest of the camp, now are you? I guess I'm stuck with you, though."

"That's not fair," Dezi joked. "You're comparing us to Willow. How could any of us be as brilliant as Mother Nature?"

"How indeed," Finkle muttered, arching his eyebrows. What little patience he had was reserved for more important things than stupidity.

"We still have a problem," Jessie commented. "How do we get in? We can't go through the fence."

"Or over it," Pete added.

"And we don't know what additional traps are lurking on the other side," Dezi mentioned, his usual jovial demeanour hiding in the face of discouragement.

Finkle dusted off a large stone and sat on the freshly cleaned space. He stretched out his stubby legs and yawned. "We watch," he explained. Leaning back, he closed his eyes. "Or, more to the point, the three of you watch. Wake me up if anything happens. I really do need my beauty rest."

"Well," Pandora groaned, "isn't this a sight? I leave you alone for a few hours and you're already sleeping on the job."

Finkle jumped, but not quite quick enough to avoid a shower of sea water from raining down over his body. "Was that really necessary?" he complained, shaking one leg which had taken the brunt of the liquid assault. "It's not like I packed a large number of suits. Unlike you, I can't ask seaweed to dress me."

"Oh, pull out your wand and stop complaining," Pandora answered, adding an eyeroll when Finkle looked the other way. "A few waves and you'll be dry again. Now... back to the problem at hand. Why are you all standing around?"

"Electric fence," Pete answered.

"I see," Pandora said. "And you followed it all the way around the property?"

"Well," Pete replied, scratching his head, "no."

"I see," Pandora said. "So, you looked for possible entrances under the fence - tunnels, perhaps?"

"Well," Pete replied, "no."

"You are sounding more like repeat than Pete," Pandora mocked. "Think about it, boys! There must be a way in and out."

"Ah, yes!" Finkle exclaimed. "We thought of that. We are waiting to see if anyone comes out." He wagged a finger at the sign. "From here we have a perfect view of the fence. I'm sure it will happen anytime now."

"And how, might I ask, do you know the way in and out is here?" Pandora questioned, folding her arms across her chest.

"Goodness, woman!" Finkle cried out. "Isn't it obvious? The sign is always on the front side of a building."

Pandora looked back at the rusted sign hanging by its last bolt. A stream of sea water flowed in the air above her head, hitting the M in Merliance. A few metal creaks later and the sign lay face-down on the ground, leaving the fence buzzing. "I don't see any sign," Pandora said, shrugging her shoulders.

"That's just great," Finkle complained. "Do tell, what has the Goddess of the Sea been doing with her time?" He added finger-made quotation marks in the air as he articulated the title. It wasn't the first time he'd expressed his disbelief in the witch's abilities, nor would it be the last.

"I have been searching the area for Mermaids," Pandora stated.

"And," Finkle said, "did you find any?"

"No," Pandora admitted. "Of course, I didn't think I would. I have been living in these oceans for many years and have yet to come across one."

"Then, I guess we all have come up empty," Finkle said. "You aren't doing any better than we are. I'm not sure that gives you the right to criticize us."

"I suppose that's true," Pandora admitted. "I, however, am not giving up. I'll look for an underwater entrance. I expect all of you to look for a way in, rather than waiting for one to find you."

Chapter Three

After the previous day, class was the last place Nadine wanted to be. Her peers weren't any different from other high school-aged students - unmercifully cruel when they smelt weakness. It didn't help that her parents had an unusual sense of humour. Here she was learning about Mermaids with a name that rhymed with sardine.

She did her best to block out the snickers and jokes when she arrived. There would be something new to hold the jests of the masses soon. Today's lesson was on mating rituals - they'd have plenty of material to laugh at.

Nadine sighed. Under normal circumstances, this was a subject she would have found quite interesting. What made it even more intriguing was the fact that there were few books on the subject that weren't taboo.

There were only a handful of mentions in terunji tales about Mermen. There was also a very good reason for that. Mermaids were, in fact, an all-female race, living quite happily in their own society without any male interaction. In order to preserve the race, every so often, some were chosen to come to shore for a mating ritual. Once they shed their tails, they had anatomies similar to terunji women - complete with reproductive systems, albeit slightly different from what one might expect.

"I thought Mermaids laid eggs," Danny snickered, knowing that if a Mermaid mating happened in the near future, he would probably be chosen for his superior physique to father a new generation. That was right up his alley - lots of fun and no strings attached. If a sign-up form appeared, his name would be the first on the list to volunteer.

"They do," Professor Jenkins answered. "But only after fertilization has taken place. They mate in the same manner as the majority of life forms we know to exist do." After a round of chuckles died down, she continued, "This is not an act of pleasure, it's a requirement for the continued survival of their species. Once the egg is laid, their scales are reproduced quickly; their tails are reformed; and they return to the sea. The egg grows in size with the embryo and resembles a large pearl just prior to hatching. The process takes centuries to complete and even then, only a small percentage of these Merchildren survive. Every egg is precious."

"Is that why bandits stole some?" Danny asked.

"We believe so," the teacher answered. "It was lucky there was a hero to put a stop to that or we might not exist today."

Nadine felt heat filling her cheeks. A mirror wasn't needed to know she was red as a lobster under the scrutiny of stares. A fleeting wish dashed through her mind - if only she were half the woman her great-grandmother had been. The voices of her classmates snapped her back to reality - she was no hero; she was merely a sardine in the sea of life. No doubt she'd end up canned in some cupboard until her expiry date passed and she was tossed away.

The bell rang. Nadine waited for the room to empty before exiting herself. She had survived enough days like that day to know lunch was going to be the real test. Her eyes studied the ground as she walked through the cafeteria, hoping that by not acknowledging anyone, they wouldn't acknowledge her. It didn't work. People can be cruel. The name calling and snickers simply intensified with her nonchalant attitude. This crowd wouldn't be satisfied until either she broke or someone else became the target.

Surveying the room, there was only one group of friends she could sit with. After only two steps in that direction, a sardine hit her tray. She froze. There was no reason to draw attention to anyone else. Instead, she found a bench outside among a group of trees.

Fresh air filled her lungs, calming her nerves, but the trembling persisted. The sides of her lips curled down, her brows matching under the weight of sadness. The lines forming between them had become frequent guests, leaving traces of their existence to mark territory to later be reclaimed.

She stared at her lunch for a few moments before gagging at the thought of eating - all signs of an appetite missing. It disappeared when the razing began and wasn't likely to return anytime soon. Forcing herself, she gulped back a container of juice, the one item that had survived becoming trash. The only thing at that moment more revolting than food was the thought of returning to classes that afternoon. There was one choice: play the sick card. No one would question her about it, especially since her marks were the best in the class - at least when it came to the intellectual side of things.

Thumbs twiddled furiously, trying to work through the details at the same time as her mind. It would be close to impossible to remain hidden for the rest of the day and yet she couldn't be seen. That meant leaving Merliance grounds - which also meant breaking more than a handful of rules. Getting caught would end the little freedom she had. It wasn't a lot, but her once-a-month trips to the amusement park made things a little more bearable. If she lost that, it was a one-way ticket to stir crazy city. No one wanted to go there.

Very few had ever tried to break in or out of Merliance. Security was supposed to be top-notch. Nadine, however, had found highly-probable flaws in the system years ago. Although she'd tried to warn the Overseers, they paid little to no attention to her. Without being addressed, those same problems still existed. It was time to put her theories to the test.

Nadine crept towards the farthest exit from any buildings and waited. There were only minutes left before class resumed. Satisfied the majority of staff and students were otherwise engaged, she turned her attention to the task before her. A handful of pebbles and dirt hit the fence, sending sparks flying. Nadine smiled. A whistling buzz meant the fence was powering down. Eyes glued to her watch, she pressed the timer precisely when the noise stopped.

Exactly forty-two seconds was all she had to open the gate and exit. Being successful meant moving faster than ever before. Her hand tingled, grabbing the wire gate a second too soon. Her eyes still watering from the stinging sensation, she bolted forward - her vision obscured. There was no need to look back. A whiff of burning hair was enough to know a few strands didn't make it, but the rest of her had. She had enough thick curls that those sacrificed wouldn't be missed.

Nadine bent over at the waist, breathing deeply. Sprinting was a new experience - one she hoped not to have to repeat too many times in her life. She wasn't by any means overweight, just clumsy. There was a certain awkwardness between her two feet that others simply didn't have or understand. That translated into an inability to perform most physical activities and, as a result, slightly underdeveloped muscles compared to the rest of her classmates.

For now, that was behind her. She glanced around, happy to be free from Merliance, at least for a little while. When nightfall crept over the land, she'd have to return. Until then, she had the whole world to explore and Mermaids weren't a part of the equation.

Chapter Four

"How, exactly, are we supposed to know if we find an entrance?" Dezi complained. "We've been walking for hours and the fence looks the same as when we started."

"That's because it is the same as when we started," Jessie answered, pointing to a lump on a rock up ahead.

"So we walked all the way around for nothing?" Pete asked, throwing his hands in the air and letting them fall back down to his sides. "That's perfect. We totally wasted an entire afternoon. We might as well have taken a nap with the Professor."

"No use complaining," Jessie stated. "What's done is done. We're back now. Let's make the most of it." He motioned for his brothers to follow him. Taking the lead came naturally to him, especially being the oldest, even if it was only by mere minutes. He was also the tallest of the triplet brothers.

Usually, children born together look identical. Not in the case of these brothers. They were each different in appearance and personality. It was almost as if they were three parts to one whole person, each getting different qualities. The only thing they shared was the light-brown shade of their hair and matching eye colour.

"Back so soon," Professor Finkle chuckled, opening one eye. "I thought you'd take at least another few hours."

"We thought you were sleeping," Pete blurted back, taking a moment to pull off one of his shoes. As it tipped over, dirt and a few pebbles fell to the ground. "With all the water that surrounds this place, you wouldn't think it would be so dry."

"Lucky we are both wrong, I suppose. As it turns out, I have been diligently watching." Finkle swung his legs off the side of his makeshift bed - sitting up in the same motion. "Perhaps now you boys will realize I know a bit more than you'd like to admit."

"Pandora did make a compelling case," Dezi argued.

"Pandora," Finkle laughed. "This is the most important advice I'll ever give you three. I expect you to listen closely." He paused long enough for the boys to gather close. "Women are trouble."

"That's it?" Dezi complained.

"Yes, that's it," Finkle stated, throwing his arms in the air. "If you let them get under your skin, they'll have you wandering around like fools for the rest of your life - just like you did today. It's even worse if you fall in love with one. After that, you won't have a moment's rest. Heed my words: women aren't worth the pain and suffering that comes part and parcel with them. Stay clear of them as much as you can."

"I don't recall you voicing that opinion when Pandora was around," Dezi commented. "You didn't complain she was joining us."

"Yes, well," Finkle started, patting the box still in his arms, "sacrifices have to be made sometimes. It wouldn't do our little quest any good having her calling me names. The three of you would be best to listen to my advice over her's in the future. It could save you another afternoon of meaningless walking."

"Be that as it may," Pete replied, "you haven't gotten any closer to finding a way in than we did."

"Not true, my boy. Not true," the Professor stated. "I've already seen someone emerge from within."

"Well, where is he?" Jessie asked, springing to his feet.

"She," Finkle answered, "is sitting on the rocks over there - just out of sight."

"And you didn't talk to her?" Jessie snarled.

"Wait!" the Professor yelled, too late. Jessie was already headed in the girl's direction, ready for an interrogation "Stupid boy. Watching her would have given us much better answers - ones we could rely on." Still grumbling, he followed.

"Hey," Jessie called out.

The girl stumbled backwards. Jessie raced to her aid. With his advanced strength and speed he easily reached her before she made contact with the ground.

Nadine squeaked, her voice lost. She glanced over her shoulder at the rocky terrain then back up at her saviour.

"Are you alright?" Jessie asked, his arms still cradling her waist. "That could have been a nasty fall." The corners of his lips curled upwards. He'd become used to the natural strength that he had been empowered with, but somehow, at that moment, it seemed accentuated. Feeling this girl tremble in his arms; seeing the lost look in her eyes; and feeling her cling to him made him feel stronger than he'd ever been before.

"I," Nadine stuttered.

"It's okay," Jessie whispered. "You're safe." He helped her to a standing position, catching her again when her legs wobbled, threatening to give out.

"Sorry," she muttered.

"Is everything okay?" Pete asked, catching up.

"Yeah," Jessie said, not taking his eyes off of her reddening face. "She'll be fine. I think I frightened her when I yelled."

"Who are you?" Nadine squeaked, her voice not yet ready to obey the commands her brain was issuing.

"I think," Professor Finkle huffed, trying to catch his breath. He placed one hand against a tall rock and the other over his chest. "The question is, who are you?" Finkle coughed, spitting out a glob of phlegm. His trusty handkerchief made its way to wipe his mouth, the flip side dabbed droplets of sweat from his brow.

"I live not too far from here," Nadine answered. "I've never seen any of you in these parts before." The only thing worse than sneaking out of a secret complex would be divulging the existence of their organization. She had trained all her life to deal with outsiders, but somehow now in the presence of this group, she was tongue-tied. In her family line, mistakes weren't allowed to be made.

"I don't recall seeing many houses near here," Finkle stated, now fully in control of his body again. He stood erect, although still allowing the rock to support part of his weight. "Whereabouts did you say you lived?"

"My mother taught me not to talk to strangers," Nadine said. "I've broken that rule already, but I'm not about to tell four men where I live."

Finkle laughed. "My dear child," he started, "if we wanted to bring harm to you, we could do so right here and now. I assure you, there is no need for us to wait and follow you to your home."

Nadine gasped. Her feet tangled, sending her stumbling backwards. Jessie's arms closed around her, stopping another nasty fall before it happened. He was taller than her by at least a foot. Turning around brought her face-first into his muscular chest - a place she hadn't anticipated being when the day began. Her knees buckled, but this time not because they were tangled.

"Are you okay?" Jessie asked, staring down at her brown eyes. There was a subtle hint of gold hidden in them that he hadn't noticed before. A sheepish grin crept over his face as her trembling ceased in his arms. "We aren't trying to frighten you. We just have a few questions."

"What do you want?" she whispered.

"We are looking for something," Jessie started. "A place called Merliance, to be exact. There was a sign on the fence over there, but it fell off."

"Merliance," Nadine repeated. "There used to be a company named that, but it hasn't been operational for years."

"Do you know when it shut down?" Finkle asked.

"No," Nadine lied. "It was before I can remember."

"Do you know who owned it?" Finkle questioned.

"No," Nadine lied again.

"It's in your backyard, so to speak, and yet you don't know anything about it?" Finkle complained. "Why is that?"

"Why would I ask about a closed-up company?" Nadine argued. "I have no interest in it. Most people from this area work at the fishery on the far shore. You could ask there. They might know."

"If this place is abandoned as you say it is, why are you walking outside its fence?" Finkle asked.

"I was walking the shoreline - following the rocks," Nadine answered. "I love the sea. This area isn't as populated as others. It allows me to think. What do you want with a closed-up factory, anyway?"

"Well, my dear," Finkle said, eyeing their detainee. He moved the box, picture forward, to his chest. "We have a few questions about something we found."

Nadine eyed the box. "What is that?" she asked. Showing her the art was an obvious trap - one she fell right into.

"That," Finkle replied, "is what we were hoping you would tell us. There's no use keeping up your little facade. I saw you emerge from within the fence."

Nadine glanced back at the fence and forward again. Her tongue darted out, leaving a touch of wetness on dry lips. Sea air was great for breathing, but not as wonderful when it came to keeping hair and skin moisturized.

Jessie studied her face, acknowledging the undeniable connection between them. He mused at the understanding of the options the girl was contemplating making. If she ran, he'd catch her; and if she screamed, it was likely no one would hear her. There was something else in her eyes as well - a fear, but not of them. A screeching of gulls above them interrupted his thoughts.

"What's inside?" Nadine asked, her voice steady and confident.

"Maps and notes in a language unknown," Finkle answered. "Can you help us?"

Nadine glanced up at the sky. Another group of birds flew overhead - indicating feeding time had arrived. Her eyes fixated on the figure of a Mermaid holding what appeared to be a pearl. Could the thieves have hidden one? Perhaps her great-grandmother had failed to return them all. "It isn't safe for you to be here," she blurted out. "You need to go. I'll meet you tomorrow. Follow the road towards town, but veer off to the left before you hit the outskirts. That road will take you to an amusement centre featuring a mini-putt golf course. Ask to go to the nineteenth hole. I'll meet you there."

"How do we know you'll show?" Jessie asked.

Nadine chuckled. "I've waited my whole life for this opportunity. I'm not about to waste it. I'll be there."

Jessie nodded. "We'll be there too."

"That's it?" Finkle complained. "You expect me to let her go? She's our only lead. We can't afford to lose her."

"She'll be there," Jessie said. "I can feel it. I think we should do what she says."

"Of course," Finkle grumbled, beginning the trek to town. "At least we can sleep in a comfortable bed for the night."

Pete slapped him on the back. "Good way to look at it, Sir."

Jessie glanced over his shoulder in time to see Nadine disappear, safely inside the fence. He shook his head. The Professor had been right again. Perhaps it was time to take the old man a little more seriously. He jogged to catch up to his brothers; they were too slow to waste any more energy than that on.

"It might be a trap," Finkle explained. "We should be prepared."

"You really think so? She doesn't seem very dangerous to me." Dezi stated, crinkling his nose. "What do you think, Jess?"

"Huh," Jessie muttered, glancing back over his shoulder again. "I think she's cute." A grin formed on his face, one that wasn't going to disappear anytime soon.

Finkle sighed. "Didn't you hear a word I said, boy? Women are trouble and you might have just put us in the middle of a world of it because you think she's cute."

Chapter Five

Frizz - the word of the day. Nadine's bottom lip jutted out as she blew air upwards, forcing a few stray curls off her forehead. Even tied back, stragglers managed to find a way loose and annoy her. With the hot weather and sea air, there was no amount of conditioner that was going to help.

She glanced out the window and sighed. Those at the top of her class were already beginning their practice sparring for the day. None of them were cursed with thick curly hair. She watched for a split second, dodging behind the heavy orange curtains to avoid being seen by Danny. She chuckled to herself. There was no way he would notice her in a window when he didn't notice her anywhere else. Her thoughts betrayed her, flashing images of the mystery guy from the day before. Why had he affected her so much?

Nadine threw herself on the bed, burying her head in a pillow to muffle a scream. A new crush wasn't what she needed, with two already existing. The first was the best friend she'd ever had. They'd grown up together. She'd fallen hard, before she even knew what falling for someone meant.

To her, Abigail was perfect in every way, although two years older. For some, a picture was needed to remind them of the features of loved ones lost. This wasn't the case for Nadine. Nothing could make her forget Abigail's perfect olive-tanned skin and greenish-hazel eyes. The last time they saw each other, they kissed - Nadine's first kiss. She rubbed a finger over her lips, remembering the sensation. Unfortunately, she was the only one who seemed to have any memory of Abigail. That was the frustrating part.

Being a part of Merliance was a life commitment. It wasn't something one could simply decide not to do anymore. So, when Abigail disappeared, Nadine assumed it meant she had been killed. What didn't add up was why all trace of her existence had been erased. Nobody, not even her parents, would talk about it. If she admitted they were right, then she wasn't just crazy, her first kiss wasn't real either. It would have meant nothing.

It was the beginning of the current year when Nadine realized how attractive Danny was. Watching him from a distance made her body tingle and thoughts wander to places she hadn't ever thought about before. That feeling was enjoyable, but nothing compared to how the new guy made her go weak in the knees. He was even there to catch her when it happened.

That, she told herself, was only part of the equation as to why she was about to risk everything to meet him again. Her mission was to find out what was in that box. If it did hold clues to a lost Mermaid egg, she was determined to be the one to find it. This was her chance to live up to her great-grandmother's legacy. This was her time to shine and show everyone she wasn't a useless piece of furniture waiting to be shoved into a dusty, dim-lit basement and forgotten.

The heel of a shoe came down on the back side of the pink pig on her dresser. "Sorry dude, looks like you're headed to the bacon factory." The figurine shattered into small pieces, her life savings strewn amidst. She pocketed a few gold and silver coins.

After an ample application of lip gloss, Nadine was ready to sneak out. The Cafe section of the amusement park was busy enough that she'd be safe, but to remain vigilant, she brought along a wand, hidden in her back pocket. She might not be proficient with a sword, but she could decently point and fire off a bit of magic. It only took a little confusion to cause a distraction big enough to make an escape.

She glanced around the room, making sure it was messy enough for anyone who might come snooping to believe she'd been ill and gone for fresh air.

"Alibi - check. Wand - check. Lip gloss - check. Money - check. Guess that's it," Nadine said to her own reflection. "You can do this!" She pulled down one of her motivational sticky notes that framed her mirror. This one demanded that she stay the course. After reading it four times, she was ready to put the advice into action.

A stray curl plopped down on her forehead again. She moaned, huffing it back off with a blast of air. After the breath was done, it bounced back down to the same spot, daring her to test its resolve. Her arms lifted up and fell back down, symbolizing the curl had won that round. There wasn't any time to worry about it. Missing the strangers wasn't part of the plan.

Chapter Six

Rustling sounds never were the best way to wake a guy up. Pete opened one eye and groaned. "What in the realms are you doing?"

"Sorry," Professor Finkle replied. "I seem to have lost something."

Pete grumbled a few choice words under his breath before sitting upright in the bed. "These wouldn't be what you are looking for?" he asked, jingling a set of keys in his hand. Professor Finkle had insisted he take care of the box during their quest for the Fountain of Youth, but Pete and his brothers took turns watching over the only thing that could open said box.

"No!" Professor Finkle exclaimed. "Of course not. We do, after all, have an agreement about the box and keys." Finkle's lips curled up into a smile that could put a con artist to shame.

"I didn't think so," Pete scoffed. "I am curious, though, what exactly are you looking for... at this early hour... in my room?"

"I was missing a few items from my bag and thought perhaps they got mixed up with someone else's things," Finkle explained. "It is an early hour and I didn't want to disturb anyone. You didn't get the chance to rest that I did yesterday... thanks to Pandora."

"Maybe I can help," Pete offered. "Which items?"

"Oh, you know, just a few personal hygiene items that might have gotten packed wrong - nothing big."

"Professor," Pete replied. "There are so many things wrong with what you just said, it's hard to know where to start... but I'll try. First, I'm not sure you use many personal hygiene items. Your teeth are a shade of yellow I have no desire to describe or see. Have you even brushed them once since you left Sleeping Sands?" His fingers brushed over shut eyelids, removing the small bits of crust left by the sandman.

"Well..."

Pete put up one hand. "You don't have to answer. Moving on, you always insist on your own room, with your own bathroom. There would be no opportunity for our things to become mixed up as you claim."

"Are you done?" Finkle asked. Using his pinky finger nail, he picked some lodged food from between his teeth and examined it. He shook his hand, sending the remnants of dinner flying against a wall. It stuck in place as if glued.

"Almost," Pete answered. "My door was locked. You had to break into this room. Even half-asleep, I know that's too much trouble for you - especially for personal hygiene items. Let's face it, washing up isn't a high priority on your list of daily chores."

Professor Finkle waved one finger in Pete's direction. "I owe you an apology. I had you pegged as being as intellectually inept as your brothers. I see now I was mistaken. I admit it. I was looking for the keys."

"Really," Pete muttered, rolling his eyes. "Big surprise."

"Oh, don't look at me like that," Finkle hissed. "I have spent my whole life researching what this box contains. You can't expect a man like me not to want to interpret those papers and maps. I couldn't sleep and thought I'd get a head start on it."

"Purely for the sake of our quest to save my sister, of course," Pete mocked.

"Of course," Finkle replied, smiling.

"Except," Pete commented, "we all have a copy of the papers inside the box. You could have gone over those."

"Don't you think I have?!" Professor Finkle yelled through grinding teeth. He cleared his throat. "I've been over the copies hundreds of times. I'm missing something - something that the copies didn't pick up. If I can just get my hands on the originals, I might be able to figure out what it is."

"I appreciate your frustration," Pete offered. "But I don't approve of your actions nonetheless. Rather than explaining it to us, you chose to try to steal. Surely, you see how that looks. I'm willing to keep this misunderstanding between you and me. I hope we won't have any further incidents to deal with."

"That's good of you, my boy," Finkle said, backtracking to the door.

"Oh, Professor," Pete called out. "That doesn't mean I trust you. I'll be watching you like a hawk. One wrong move and... well, I'm not without abilities of my own."

Finkle's expression mutated into a scowl. "I'm very much aware of what you and your brothers can do. Look at it this way, if I hope to make it to the Fountain of Youth in one piece, I need you boys and the sea witch. I have no plans of attempting what I know is a difficult journey by myself."

The door slammed.

Chapter Seven

Dezi glanced at his brothers, then back at the sign, *Whacky Wild Mini-Putt & Amusement.* "Are we sure this is the place?" he asked, wondering where the actual course was hiding. He eyed the fading paint and weeds growing in the lot surrounding the building. Even the one door, shaped to resemble a clown's mouth, was missing a few teeth.

"Do you see any other mini-golf places?" Finkle sighed, pushing passed the three brothers. "Hurry up."

"Like I have to move fast to catch up to you," Jessie mumbled under his breath, watching the short man waddle inside.

Dezi laughed, patting his brother on the back. "Come on. Let's not keep the Professor waiting. We wouldn't want to upset him." The truth was, the Professor was wearing thin on all of their nerves.

"What exactly is mini-putt?" Jessie asked, following his brothers.

"Not sure," Pete replied, shaking his head. "But I think we are about to find out."

"We should be fine. It's a terunji game of some sort," Dezi explained. "How hard can it be?" He held the door open, gesturing with one hand for his brothers to enter ahead of him.

The inside of the building wasn't in much better shape, looking more like a temporary shop set up for illegal transactions than a family fun centre.

"How can I help?" a man asked from behind the counter. He shifted his jaw from side to side, making annoying popping noises.

"My boys and I would like to play a little mini-putt," the Professor announced, producing an over-exaggerated wink at the end.

The man alternated glances between the four, all the while rubbing the two-day old stubble that shadowed his thin face. He glanced back down at a magazine on the counter, apparently unimpressed by any of them. "Over there," he said, pointing to a wall covered with bins of different coloured golf balls.

"We'd like nine..."

"Over there," the man repeated, slightly louder.

Pete ushered Finkle away from the front of the building. If there was one thing he had learnt since this journey began, it was that the Professor had a bit of a temper. The red colour flooding into Finkle's face, meant he was about to say something they'd all regret. They hadn't brought him along just to continually clean up after the toxic spew that could leak from his mouth at any given moment. Being cocky when the four of them were alone was one thing - in public was another.

"You should have let me give that attendant a piece of my mind," Finkle complained, grinding his teeth.

"That," Pete answered, "would be counter-productive. If we get thrown out of here, we won't find out anything."

"Fine," the Professor agreed. "But don't expect me to be full of pleasantries on my way out."

Dezi snorted a chuckle, watching Jessie stand perfectly still, his arms crossed over his chest - chin cupped in one hand. "Check it out," he said, nodding in his brother's direction. "There's some deep thought happening there."

"Not worried the strong man will over hear you?" Finkle asked, raising an eyebrow. "I would imagine he could turn the two of you into mush easily."

"Jessie's not listening," Pete answered. "Check out the scowl on his face. He's way in there. Lost in the confines of his own mind." His eyes widened as his arms separated in front of him.

"You mean lost in space." Dezi laughed, letting out another snort.

"If you two are done with your sibling razzing," Finkle complained, "perhaps we can get to our meeting on time?"

Jessie shifted his weight, letting out a sigh. "Do you think we just pick any colour?" He picked up a red ball and tossed it in the air. "Heads up," he called out.

Dezi reached up and caught it. "I am partial to red," he commented, snickering. "And I am a perfect ten." He turned the ball in his fingers so the others could see the number printed on it. "Are they all numbered?"

Jessie grabbed a second ball. "The red ones all have ten marked on them."

"The green say nine," Pete said, holding another ball up in the air. "Maybe we have to add them up to make the number of holes we are going to be playing?"

"We can't play more than one ball each," Finkle announced, grabbing the green and red balls and throwing them back. "Is there a nineteen on any?"

"There is one through ten and an eighteen," Pete replied, scratching his head. "No nineteen."

"There must be a pattern," Jessie said, his eyebrows pressing inwards, forming the beginnings of a new scowl. He threw his hands in the air. "It doesn't make any sense. Why not just give us the balls we need?"

"Don't strain yourself," Dezi said, smiling.

"I can't believe I am about to say this, but I fully understand your brother's frustration," Finkle admitted. "There's a salesperson here for a reason. He should be telling us what to do if he wants to make a sale."

"Maybe he's like the bus driver in Pewterclaw was," Dezi said, juggling three brightly-coloured golf balls.

"Bus driver?" Finkle questioned.

"Yeah, he was not only a bus driver. His job was to keep people out of the City that didn't belong there." The three balls crashed to the ground, knocking over a display sign. "Whoops," Dezi cringed, picking up the cardboard. "Wait a second. The sign says: *Pick your balls carefully. They add up to all the fun you are looking for.*"

"Need I remind you," Finkle stated, "we are not here for enjoyment purposes!"

"Funny thing," Dezi replied, "I had already figured that out. Look at the picture. There is a family of three and the numbers on their balls equal eighteen. I don't know a lot about the sport, but I read up a little bit about it last night. I'm pretty sure eighteen holes is a normal round of golf."

"I don't know which I am surprised more about," Finkle exclaimed, "the fact you have made a valid point without joking or that you can read." He cackled.

The three brothers exchanged glances - none of them inspired by the Professor's attempt at wit.

"There are four of us. We need four numbers that add to nineteen," Pete said, pushing passed the Professor to the bins. The last comment had earned Finkle the silent treatment. It was one thing for brothers to make fun of each other, but another for an outsider to try it. In his opinion, the man was lucky the three of them didn't put him in his place. If there was one thing all three brothers took seriously, it was family. That should have been obvious given it was the reason behind the quest they were currently on.

"I have a ten," Jessie announced.

Pete tossed a ball in the air. "Look alive."

"Number one," Dezi said, a smile fighting its way back onto his face.

"I'll take three," Pete announced. "Because I was born third." He tossed another ball over his head without looking.

"Ow!" Finkle complained, rubbing his temple.

"Your ball is number five," Pete stated. "Better pick it up." He led the way to the counter, not waiting for a complaint.

The four balls rolled on the flat surface, coming to rest against the magazine. Sunken eyes peered up at the four. The attendant raised his upper lip, forming an imperfect letter M. "All four balls must play all holes. Putters are outside - pick what you want. Follow the signs." He pressed a button under the counter and the back wall opened.

A rush of wind howled, rattling the building's metal exit, bits of rust shaking off as it did. A reddish brown coloured powder littered the ground.

"Thank you," Pete said, not expecting an answer.

Jessie ducked, barely avoiding a second gust lifting the dust. Finkle wasn't so lucky, receiving the brunt of the blast directly into his open mouth, silencing any complaints he might have had.

The Professor spat on the floor before stepping outside. Even his handkerchief was covered in rust particles. He tossed it in a garbage can, choosing to use a ball wash towel to clean his face. With his vision restored, he smirked at the course. Every hole appeared to be some deranged form of common terunji nursery rhyme. The first one was a reproduction of a classic.

A large egg sat on a brick wall - legs dangling down, swinging in the wind. As they moved from one side to the other, a hole appeared in the wall - only slightly bigger than their golf balls.

"I'll go first," Finkle announced. "Looks easy enough to figure out what we have to do here."

"What, exactly, is it we have to do?" Jessie enquired.

"According to what I read, we need to hit our ball with one of these clubs," Dezi explained. "The object is to use as few hits as you can to sink the ball in a small hole."

Jessie cranked his head in his brother's direction. "You're kidding," he replied, raising one lip. "Why would anyone want to do that?"

"For fun!" Finkle bellowed. "Now watch me." He licked a finger and held it up. "Uh-huh." He looked down at the ball already on the well-worn, fake-green turf. Placing both hands on his club, he took a wide stance, wiggling his bottom as he set his feet the way he wanted them. He watched the legs swing, counting each pass before bringing the club back. The ball spun on impact, hurdling towards the wall. A piece of eggshell fell, blocking its path.

"Good realms!" Finkle exclaimed. "We must have to finish the hole before that character cracks up."

"That pun was a little better," Dezi laughed. "Let's do this thing. He whacked at his ball without taking any time to prepare a stance. It drifted through the small passageway, clearing the wall easily. "See you on the flip-side." He fired off a wink. With the putter slung over his shoulder, he disappeared around the side.

Pete followed a similar pattern. A second piece of eggshell barely missed his ball as it trickled through to join his brother's. "Phew, that was close. Watch the shells, they seem to be falling faster." Another piece hit the ground, shattering into several smaller pieces.

"Piece of cake," Jessie replied. For him, sports came naturally, no matter how silly he found some of them. He tapped the ball in a sideways direction, banking it off the side bricks. He whistled sound effects as it knocked against a larger piece of shell and ricocheted directly through an opening. "Bullseye!"

"Hole-in-one!" Dezi yelled.

"Yes!" Jessie made a fist and pulled it into his body. He could still hear the Professor cursing when he joined his brothers. "Sounds like he's going to be a while. You two might as well finish up while we wait."

"Good plan," Dezi said, knocking his ball into the hole. He squatted down to retrieve it and glance through the opening at the same time. "I hope he makes it before that egg comes crashing down." The sound of a ball spinning in the cup beside him caught his attention. "Good shot, Pete." Dezi grabbed the ball and tossed it over his shoulder without looking. "Do we move on or wait?"

"I think we better wait," Pete suggested. "If these holes are timed, we may have to get through them together. The Professor is going to need as much leeway as we can give him to get through all nineteen."

"Good point," Dezi laughed.

A ball emerged, barely clearing the wall. A crash of egg shell landed on top of it, scarcely having the chance to settle before a red-faced Professor emerged in hot pursuit.

"More egg shell," Finkle huffed, a few droplets of sweat streaming down his face. Four more attempts and the ball plonked in the cup.

"Bravo!" Dezi exclaimed, clapping his hands. "How many strokes?"

"Is that necessary?" the Professor whined.

"It's electronic," Dezi said, pointing towards a lit up scorecard mounted on a stick. "I think we better be honest, too. It might not let us in wherever it is we are going if we aren't." A chuckle threatened to escape his throat. He coughed, muffling the noise, his face telling the story of the attempted cover-up.

Finkle sighed, his shoulders hanging down. "Very well," he mumbled. "Twenty-two."

"I'm sorry!" Jessie yelled. "I didn't hear you. My score was one and yours was... how many?"

"Twenty-two!" the professor yelled, grabbing the towel at the next hole's ball wash to wipe his face. "Twenty-two!" His teeth made a grinding noise. "Are you happy?" He crossed his arms over his chest, an obvious pout taking over, replacing the signs of anger.

"So who goes first?" Dezi asked. "I think it goes best score first and worst score last." He laughed.

"Very funny," Finkle snarled. "Let's concentrate on getting through the rest of this nightmare land."

"Anyone have a clue what we are doing on this one?" Jessie asked. "It looks rather straightforward."

"There must be a twist to it," Pete commented, glancing at the Professor.

"Oh, so now you want my help," he snickered.

"If you want, I can hit the ball and start whatever timer there is going," Jessie offered. "I'm not to blame if we fail, though."

"No need to be hasty," Finkle bellowed. "Let's see - we have a rather ugly girl... sitting on a footstool... having lunch."

"We can see that," Pete scoffed. "Do you know what could happen or not?"

"While I have read many terunji tales," Finkle stated, "I don't profess to be an expert. Give me a moment to think. I seem to remember a rhyme where a girl was eating strange food and a spider appeared beside her."

"If a spider was to be beside her, it would cover the hole," Pete observed. "We'd never be able to finish."

"Only one way to find out!" Jessie declared. "Get your balls ready, boys." The club swatted at the ground. As soon as his ball finished one full rotation, a spider descended on a thread, landing on top of the hole. The ball hit the critter straight on, making it jump back an inch. Jessie scratched his head, letting out a big breath of air with a huff. The spider wasted no time crawling its way back over the hole.

"Now what?" Dezi asked.

"We work together," Pete announced. "Jessie's ball moved the spider a bit. If we hit it with force we can knock it off the hole. We'll have to time it right to make sure everyone gets finished before it climbs back again."

"Indeed," Finkle said, staring at the eight-legged creature. "I'll let you boys retrieve the balls."

"You aren't afraid of a spider, are you?" Dezi laughed, hitting his ball as hard as he could. The spider jerked backwards.

Pete followed suit, wasting no time firing his ball at the spider. "Professor, get this one in and redeem yourself for the last hole."

"No pressure," Finkle replied, wiggling his bottom into position. He pulled his club back and swung through. The ball coasted in the direction of the hole, but was blocked by one hairy leg jutting out.

"Jessie," Pete said. "Nail that thing hard."

"No problem," Jessie replied, smiling. He lifted his club and whacked the ball with force into the mid-section of the spider. A lucky bounce found it spinning in the hole. It disappeared as a sign popped up, indicating players could find their balls waiting for them on the next tee.

"Dezi," Pete said. "Hit it to the side. We need to make sure the Professor can get his shot in before we finish."

"One clear shot and it will go in," Finkle stated.

Dezi wasted his turn, knocking the spider clear. The statue-like girl's head jerked up as she let out a blood-curdling scream.

"Not near the girl!" Finkle yelled. "If she runs away, the rhyme is over."

Pete grabbed his club and smacked his ball, forcing the spider away from the girl and her lunch. Her head bobbed back down, springs in her neck making the movement appear mechanical. He wiped his brow. "That was close. Professor, hurry." A ball hit the cup before he finished his request.

Dezi's ball was already spinning towards the spider. "Get ready, Pete. Get yours in quick so I have a shot."

Pete's ball barely hit the cup when Dezi's followed. The spider crawled back up to its web, hanging above.

"Onwards," Dezi cheered. "Hole three awaits."

"I wouldn't be so excited," Jessie said, pointing towards a large bridge. "I have a strange feeling that bridge is going to collapse."

"Right you are, my boy," Finkle said, patting him on the back. "Most likely when that lady makes her way into the middle. I believe as winner, you're up next." He laughed. "Whoever put this course together had a strange sense of humour."

Chapter Eight

The Professor wiped his brow with his sleeve. A large tree blocked the way to the eighteenth hole. "I'd be happy to never think about another nursery rhyme again in my life. I never realized how creepy they all really are until today. To think the magical authorities actually consider us a threat to the psyche of the terunji. I'd say they are already a disturbed race. These children's tales are enough to frighten anyone."

"Professor," Pete said. "I hate to disturb you, but we only have two holes left. We may still make it before afternoon."

"Right," Finkle answered. "I'm looking forward to sitting down and not moving for a very long time."

"I guess we need to go around the tree," Jessie stated.

"Yes," Finkle replied. "Before that baby falls."

"Baby?!" Dezi screamed. "What baby?"

"Up there in the cradle," Finkle answered. "I remember this one because I thought it was odd a mother would tell her child that a baby was going to fall from a treetop. I expect the wind to start blowing as soon as the first ball is struck. It will rock the cradle until it turns upside down, allowing poor Jimmy or Jill to fall out and crash onto the ground."

"The terunji are messed-up people," Pete said, staring at the cradle.

"No arguments there," Finkle stated.

"If the wind is blowing that hard, it could affect the ball's direction as well," Jessie said.

"That actually makes sense." Finkle applauded.

"I'm not all brawn and good looks," Jessie snickered. He placed his ball on the ground and aimed it to the side of the tree. "We have to aim left. You can tell by the angle the cradle is sitting the wind has to blow the opposite way to make it fall." The ball launched, spinning left. The wind blew, forcing its trajectory back towards the right. The ball hit the hole and fell in. "And the crowd goes wild." He threw his hands in the air.

The remaining three followed his lead, finishing the hole before the baby so much as fussed.

"The nineteenth hole - shall we recap what we have learnt today?" Finkle asked.

"I'd rather not," Jessie replied. "Let's just finish. What's up with the circle of dead bodies? Are we supposed to putt around them?"

"Your guess is as good as mine," Finkle replied.

"We are going in blind like the mice on hole fifteen," Dezi chuckled. "Slapshot away. I suppose I could bank it off a body and in."

"Just get on with it," Finkle ordered.

"Hey," Dezi complained. "This is my one chance at going first. I plan to make the most of it." He imitated the Professor's butt wiggle before hitting his ball into the circle of bodies. It bounced off three before stopping within two inches of the hole.

"Nice shot," Jessie praised, patting his brother's back. He placed his ball on the ground and made a similar swing, but ended up on the opposite side to his brother. "Last hole and I think we're getting the hang of this game."

"I think we are becoming desensitized." Pete argued, placing his ball on the tee. "Those are dead bodies we are aiming at." His ball rolled to a stop between two heads.

"They aren't real," Finkle said, taking his stance. He swung and the ball hit an eye, sending liquid flying.

"If it isn't real," Pete argued, "those are pretty good special effects."

"The smell is raunchy like dead bodies too," Jessie commented, wrinkling up his nose. Breathing through his mouth wasn't much better, offering a taste of death in place of the scent.

Pete sunk his ball. "Ugh. Hurry up. I'd like to get out of here. I should have worn some cologne to sniff."

"Oh, good gracious," Finkle said as he sunk the last ball of the four. "That's what rhyme this is." The bodies burst into flames around them, trapping them in the middle. "Get ready to fall down!" Finkle screamed as the floor gave way.

"Looks like we made it inside," Dezi said, rolling onto his back. The large mat underneath them had cushioned part of the fall, but there would still be bruises to commemorate their day at *Whacky Wild Mini-Putt & Amusement.*

"Yeah," Jessie agreed. "But inside where?"

Finkle groaned. "There is only one way to go," he said, a shaky finger pointing towards a bright red door. It was hard to miss, considering it made a glaring contrast against the grey walls and floor of the rest of the room. "One of you lads be a good fellow and help an old man to his feet, please."

Jessie extended and arm, pulling the Professor up. A series of cracking noises accompanied his movements.

"Professor," Dezi said. "Are you okay?"

"Yes. Yes," Finkle replied, twisting his back from side to side. "The bones are a bit old and tend to rattle a lot. I'll be fine. Let's finish our quest." He hobbled towards the door and tugged on the handle.

Chapter Nine

Dezi laughed. It was as if they had been transported into another world. This was sensory overload. The same bright colours of the golf balls were painted in every nook and cranny possible. Loud ringing bells sounded from arcade games, the noise only outweighed by laughter. A sweet smell of fresh baked goods filled the air. Cinnamon swirled around their senses before settling back down on the warm sticky buns it came from.

"Over there," Finkle said, pointing to a round booth where the mystery girl from the previous day was seated.

"Huh?" Dezi muttered, distracted by a sudden whiff of fresh cotton candy. The delectable sugary scent took its time dancing around his nose - daring him to follow to the cashier. Payment in-hand, he was already moving in the wrong direction, when the Professor redirected his shoulders.

"This way," the Professor said. "These places use magicks to enhance the scent of items. Keep your guard up, or you'll part with all your assets. You could say amusement parks and fun centres are legalized cons."

"I was wondering if you would be showing up," Nadine commented.

"That course we had to play wasn't the easiest to finish," Pete replied. "One wrong move and we could have taken even longer."

"You played it?" Nadine asked, turning the straw in the glass in front of her.

She'd ordered the *Drink of Every Flavour*. As the liquid swirled, it changed from one colour to the next - each representing a different experience that satisfied even the most finicky of sweet tooths. When one came to the flavour desired, one simply stopped stirring and drank. She picked a pastel pink which rewarded her palate with a burst of strawberry shortcake. Taking a sip, she savoured the taste before twirling the straw again, moving it more quickly to pass by some of the less appealing choices.

There had been a time when she questioned why they made some of the flavours. That was before she had been allowed to make weekend trips to town. Having a chance to meet new people gave her insight. There were diverse tastes in this realm, both magic and terunji. She didn't have the right to dictate what one person liked or didn't. That was the whole point behind the drink - although she doubted many people considered it as deeply as she had.

"You told us to," Finkle complained.

"No," Nadine argued. "I told you to ask for the nineteenth hole, not to play them. There is a big difference."

Dezi slapped his hand against his forehead. "You mean there is a way to get here directly from the front store?"

"Of course," Nadine chuckled.

"Do tell," Professor Finkle said, tapping his fingertips together, "why didn't the attendant mention it?"

"I suppose because you asked to play," Nadine answered. "You can't blame Harv. He hadn't seen you before and he is quite shy."

"Brilliant!" Finkle exclaimed.

Nadine turned her head. The full view of Professor Finkle's broken, yellow teeth was too much to handle. Interrupting someone mid-sentence wasn't her normal behaviour, but in this case, she decided it was better than allowing another word, carrying the scent of decay, to escape his mouth.

"We have limited time," she commented. "We should make the most of it. Can I see the contents of the box?"

The professor's mouth closed, perfecting a scowl. He slid the box on the clear table, side-eyeing the boys to see who had possession of the key.

"It's beautiful," Nadine mumbled. The tips of her fingers outlined the detailed carvings. She winced at the sight of her nails. Against the smooth clean lines of the artist's paint, one could tell she was a nail-biter. The uneven edges stuck out leaving to question if she had any right handling such a piece in the first place.

"Here," Pete said, the keyring jingling in his fingers. He pulled the box closer. The lid flung open, revealing the contents within. "We can't decipher the writing and have no idea what the maps are all about."

Nadine's head nodded at each piece she pulled out of the box. She rubbed her neck, choosing her words carefully. "We need to bring up a map of this realm. Clear off the table so we can see it."

"What for?" Jessie asked. "Is there a reference centre in this place too?"

Nadine laughed, but avoided his eye contact. She wasn't about to lose control now, when she was so close to doing something worthwhile - something even her great-grandmother would have been proud of. "A lot of writers come here. The tables are equipped with all the benefits of library resources and the internet." Pressing a button under the table, it lit up. A virtual keyboard appeared. A few strokes of the keys transformed the surface to a detailed map of the whole realm. "There." She crossed her arms over her chest and nodded - proud of her accomplishment.

"How does that help?" Dezi asked.

Nadine held up one of the maps. "See how it is printed on a clear material? That's so you can overlay it on top of another map to match up locations." At least she hoped that was what it was for.

"How did you know that?" Jessie asked.

"I came across it once while doing research," Nadine explained. "Pirates used it as means of hiding their most precious treasures."

"Do you think pirates are involved?" Finkle asked.

"Yes," Nadine answered, pushing the clear map around until it matched the one beneath. "That's it!" It fit over top perfectly like a singular piece of a jigsaw puzzle finally being placed to complete the picture.

"It really does match," Dezi commented. "I guess that big X is where we need to look. It seems to be underwater, though."

"Harder to find," Finkle replied. "What about the writing, can you decipher it?"

"Not with the resources that are here," Nadine answered, shaking her head. "This isn't a language I have seen before. It might even be code."

"I thought you said this place had all the resources needed," Finkle complained.

"For writing a novel!" Nadine exclaimed. "Not for deciphering an aged pirate's scribblings."

"Are there any authors even in here?" Finkle snapped.

"Yes," Nadine barked back. "A very famous one - right over there." Her finger directed their views towards a corner table with poor lighting.

"All I see is a really big otter," Dezi snickered.

"That otter is a very famous novelist around here," Nadine stated. "He comes here when he needs to get away and let loose."

"An otter?" Dezi repeated.

"An otter shifter, of course," Nadine explained. "When he gets deep into his writing he shifts. It's easier to come here as an otter than be somewhere more public when it happens."

"I can see how that would be a problem," Finkle commented. "What does he write about?"

"He's marvellous," Nadine cooed. "He writes about stuff that can happen in our world. The terunji eat it up as fantasy."

"If he is in the form of a rather large otter, how do you know it is him?" Pete asked, staring at the speed his paws were moving over a keyboard.

"His hair, of course," Nadine replied. "He has the best hair I've ever seen. I'd know it anywhere. Just look at how thick and luxurious it is. I'm surprised he doesn't do commercials for some shampoo. Someone must have asked him to."

Jessie glanced over. "He does have great hair... for an otter." His head turned back towards the food counter.

"I'm in otter disbelief that someone could have such great hair," Dezi joked, chuckling after.

"Honestly, Dez," Pete replied, "you otter be ashamed of yourself using such lame puns. I'm glad I have an otter brother."

"As the king of lame, you otter know," Dezi retorted.

"That's otter nonsense," Pete chuckled back.

"Please tell me I don't have to listen to otter puns for the rest of the day," Finkle mumbled, smacking one hand against his forehead.

"I'd love to listen to more," Nadine said, her white teeth exposed in a grin, "but I have to go."

"Then you best get otter here," Dezi said, pointing one finger in her direction. He fired off a wink.

"Follow the map," Nadine ordered. "When you have the pearl, bring it to me. I'll be waiting."

"How do we know you'll help us?" Finkle questioned.

"If you don't want my help..."

"We do," Jessie blurted out.

"If you give me the papers, I can try to decipher them while you are gone," Nadine offered.

"No papers!" Finkle exclaimed. "Handing them over would be the same as giving you the maps. We aren't about to be that trusting, especially when we don't even know your name."

"Nadine," she replied, chuckling. "I completely forgot we hadn't introduced ourselves. I guess I figured you otter know already."

Dezi laughed. "Good one. I'm Dezi and these two are my brothers, Pete and Jessie. The grump over there is Professor Finkle. Don't worry about him. One way or an otter, we'll be back with that pearl." His eyebrows waggled.

Nadine covered her mouth, a giggle escaped, but full laughter remained hidden. She almost felt as if being herself was good enough around them - like she belonged. That was something she hadn't ever felt before. Some people struggled a lifetime to find the meaning of life - to her it was simple... finding that place where she was meant to be - a piece to a puzzle that only she could fill.

"I was hoping to save some time," Nadine mumbled. "If you don't trust me, I understand." She felt the lump forming in her throat grow with every word.

She turned to leave, hiding evidence of disappointment shadowing her face. Eventually, she would have to tell them she was using them. She glanced back. "Thank you for meeting me." Her feet propelled her forward, first into a brisk pace, then, once outside the doors, to a jog. She didn't even notice she never tripped once in the process.

"And she's otter here," Dezi said, watching the door slam closed. "Do you think we upset her?"

"You three go find the pearl," Jessie ordered. "I'm going to follow Nadine. We'll meet up when you get back."

"Here we go," Finkle complained. "Didn't I warn you women were trouble? Take my advice: stay away from her.

You've got that glossed-over look in your eyes that has led to the downfall of many a man."

"It's not that," Jessie lied. "I'm the only one with the speed needed to clear the gate at the same time as Nadine. I can get inside. Like it or not, the answers we need are inside that fence. I can take a copy of the writings and maybe find a way to decipher them as well."

"It's not a bad idea," Pete agreed. "If she is using us, Jessie can find out. I'm all for it." He looked up to see an empty spot where his brother had previously been.

"You look like an otter fool," Dezi laughed. "In otter news, seems like it's just the three of us."

"Four," Finkle stated. "Let's go find the sea-witch."

"I thought women were trouble," Pete mocked.

"They are," Finkle replied. "We are one man down and need to move quickly across an ocean. I'll have to take the hag's help on this one."

"You otter be careful calling her a hag," Dezi laughed. "You otter know she has a temper."

"I'd rather her wrath right now than listen to anymore otter puns," the Professor admitted, already heading towards the door.

Chapter Ten

Nadine stood in front of the gate. It was time to disarm the defences again. A fistful of pebbles hurled through the air, sending sparks from the fence flying. Just as her dreaded short sprint began, a cool breeze nearly knocked her off-balance. She stumbled through, falling to her knees on the other side. The air that had been trapped in her lungs, afraid to escape and cause her to falter further, flowed free, piggybacking on a single hiccup. "That was close," she mumbled, not expecting an answer.

"Yeah," Jessie replied. "You totally almost didn't make it."

Nadine rolled over. Her gaze locked on the handsome boy towering over her, hand outstretched to help her up. A knight, maybe not in shining armour, but nonetheless a knight. She covered her mouth, hiding her dropped jaw. The lump forming in her throat wasn't from a crush this time - he shouldn't have been there. As soon as anyone found out a stranger was inside Merliance, there was bound to be a realm of trouble.

"What are you doing?" she whispered, staggering to her feet on her own ability. "You can't be here."

"Too late," Jessie replied. "What's the big deal? I brought the papers and thought we could decipher them together."

"You don't understand," Nadine complained. "No one comes into Merliance. There are a million rules we are breaking by simply standing here. If anyone finds out, I don't even know what will happen."

"Too late!" a male voice exclaimed.

Nadine shielded her eyes, trying to manage a glimpse at who was standing behind three large lights shining directly into their faces.

"Save your breath," the guard demanded. "You can say whatever it is you want to the Overseers in the morning."

Nadine gasped. She'd never even met an Overseer before. They were the oldest and most respected citizens, who kept things the way they should be. Their job was no easy task - making sure Merliance functioned and remained a secret. She turned her attention to Jessie. Even having known him for such a short time, she knew from the way he was carrying himself that he was planning to try an escape.

"Don't," Nadine pleaded, taking his hand. "There is nowhere to go. It's best if we face this head-on."

He nodded, squeezing her hand. "Alright," he replied. "I'm sure the Overseers are reasonable."

Nadine replied with a meek smile that faded quickly. A guard grabbed her arm, tight enough to leave a mark, pulling her forward. Her feet twisted, almost sending her back to the ground.

"I heard you were a smart one," one guard snickered.

"Not smart enough to be caught doing something like this," a second guard replied, pushing her in the middle of her back.

"Not athletic, either." He laughed. "I don't think it matters how intelligent she is. Even with all night to figure out what to say, I doubt anyone will bother to listen. It's going to break her parents' hearts when we have to tell them she's been arrested a traitor... especially in her family."

Nadine's eyes burned, holding back tears. "I'm not a traitor," she blurted out. "I haven't done anything wrong." She sniffled, taking in a deep breath. She'd never considered bravery to be one of her traits, but then again she'd never been in a situation the required her to be brave. She mustered every ounce of will in her bones to keep back her building sadness. There wasn't much she could do about things at the moment, but she wasn't going to make it worse by crying like a baby - at least not in front of anyone. Once she was alone, tears could be her companion for the night.

Chapter Eleven

"How long does she think we can sit around waiting for her?" the Professor complained. "We have a journey to make." He let out a loud huff with his breath. "Women! You can't trust them. They are always late and mess up everything."

Pete stretched out on a rock, supporting his head on one hand propped up by his elbow. "She isn't going to show up at all if you keep talking like that."

"We should have brought the otter," Dezi smirked. "He could have gone for a swim and had a better chance of finding Pandora than us."

The sound of choppy waves, bashing fists of growing anger against rocks, intensified. The swelling sea splashed up over top of them, misting down warnings - something was coming. The wind howled its own cautions in harmony with the rolling water - a music hated by those who lived by the rules of nature. The lingering odour of fish began to dissipate, making way for the foreboding scent of a coming storm.

The ocean's water crashed below them once again, this time sending a splash high in the air. The salty liquid drizzled down on the other side of the three. Droplets found each other, joining to form larger pools of liquid, each reflecting silver back towards the sky. They continued to combine - twisting and turning, until forming the outline of a woman's body.

A foot hit the ground, turning a creamy colour. As if paint had been added to her veins, the rest of the woman's body followed. Turquoise strands exploded from another splash of water, forming hair, eyebrows and lashes. Seaweed crept up the side of the steep bluff's edge, before winding up the woman's leg, forming a body suit. In an instant, the waters calmed - no sign of turmoil to be found. The sky, however, remained shadowed - a reminder of the storm still lurking nearby.

"I'm back!" Pandora exclaimed. "Did you miss me?"

"Not in the least," the Professor replied, crossing his arms over his chest.

"Oh, really?" Pandora chuckled. "I could have sworn I heard my name, but if you don't need me..."

"We need you," Pete blurted out.

"Of course you do," Pandora said. "I found a way in. There is a tunnel underwater that leads to a river inside that complex. I haven't figured out how to take all of you with me, though."

"Never mind that," Finkle commanded. "We need to go across the ocean."

"Across the ocean," Pandora repeated. "What in the realms for? I thought the place you were looking for was here."

"We need to find a hidden pirate's stash," Dezi explained. "And bring the contents back here."

"Let's be on our way, then!" Pandora exclaimed. "Wait a minute. Aren't we missing someone - the tall, strong one?"

"Honestly, woman," Finkle complained. "You call yourself a Goddess? You need to keep up. Jessie has gone inside the complex to wait for us. We are on a tight timeline, so we need to get a move on. Now, where can we find a boat?"

"How am I supposed to know what you boys did while I wasn't about?" Pandora barked. "If you need a boat, I suggest borrowing one of those." She pointed to a harbour barely visible in the distance.

"By borrow, you mean steal?" Pete asked.

"It's only stealing if we don't bring it back," Pandora explained. "With this storm coming, no one will miss it. We'll have to be quick if we want to get it back in time without being discovered."

"Well, then," Finkle said through a crooked smile. "Lead on, my lady. We will follow in your footsteps."

"How about you boys just climb down the rocks and wait?" Pandora offered. "I'll bring the boat round." She pointed to a pier.

The Professor managed to climb down only one rock before sliding onto his rear. He belted out a few cuss words with little regard for who might be in earshot.

"Did I mention it might be a bit slippery?" Pandora mocked. "There's something about sea water that makes rough edges smooth."

Chapter Twelve

Jessie bolted upright, banging his head against the bottom of the top bunk. It was the only piece of furniture in the dismal, grey room that had been his home for the evening. He rubbed the forming lump, ignoring the noise that had startled him.

"On your feet," a guard ordered.

Jessie jumped up, banging his head again as he did. "Ow!" He probably deserved that knock for forgetting the door unlocking was what disturbed him in the first place. Pain had an odd way of changing a person's train of thoughts.

"Did the spy hurt his head?" the guard mocked.

"Yeah," Jessie replied, not letting on that he could have easily escaped from the cell he was locked up in. His speed and strength were unmatched in any realm. The only reason he hadn't was because of Nadine. He liked her - a lot. It wasn't a feeling he was used to, but one he hoped to make stronger. The only way to do that was to be closer to her. In the meantime, it was probably best not to make any more trouble in case she ended up being blamed.

"Let's go," the guard demanded. "The Overseers are waiting."

Jessie sighed. "I don't suppose you'd let a guy shave and shower before meeting them?" He wasn't sure exactly what an Overseer was, but assumed they must be the leaders in Merliance.

The guard laughed. "Move," he ordered, poking the top of a spear in his prisoner's side. "They don't like to be kept waiting."

Jessie chuckled under his breath. People in power never liked to be kept waiting. That was a statement that probably didn't need to be made, and yet every guard or officer always used it. Something original would have been a nice change of pace. Merliance was turning out to be like every other secret organization out there - far too preoccupied with its own importance. If half of them took the time to think about working together, the realms would be a better place. Far too much time was spent undermining what the other was doing.

Jessie's toes flinched, his feet unhappy with the cold floor in the hallway. For some reason, the guards had taken his shoes and socks when he first arrived. Without a blanket, they had been cold all night. He glanced down and sighed at the unusual colour setting in. It wasn't frigid enough for frostbite, but perfect for discomfort.

"Turn left!" the guard demanded, prodding him with spear again.

"Ow!" Jessie exclaimed, turning the corner. "You don't have to jab me. Ask and I'll turn." He froze at the entrance to a circular room. A single path led to the centre, where two chairs had been positioned. Nadine sat in one... the other remained vacant.

"Please take a seat," a man requested from behind one of the desks arranged in a semi-circle formation at the front of the room.

Jessie complied. "Are you okay?" he whispered. Nadine didn't answer. He glanced down at her dainty feet, wondering if the guards had taken her shoes as well. A short-lived smile flashed over his lips at the sight of tiny happy faces painted on her toe nails. The novelty of her pedicure was quickly overcome by the realization that Nadine's toes were likely as cold as his.

"You are here today because you have broken numerous rules and endangered the secrecy of this organization," one man stated. "Nadine, how do you plead to the charge of treason?"

The door flew open. "Lawrence! Why wasn't I summoned?" Nadine's father bellowed. "I have a right to be present for any proceeding involving my family. This is preposterous."

"Charles," Lawrence replied. "I was merely trying to save you the embarrassment of facing all of us. I know what a blow this must be for you. If you would like to stay, please take a seat."

"I'd like to do more than stay," Charles stated. "I will speak on my daughter's behalf. There has obviously been a mistake."

"No, father," Nadine cried, standing. "I will speak for myself. I made a mistake and I deserve to be punished in any way the Overseers see fit."

"Wait a minute," Jessie complained. "Nadine didn't do anything. I am the one who broke into your compound."

Nadine squared her stance to Jessie. "I am the one who left the grounds. If I hadn't done that, none of this would have happened."

"You didn't know we were out there and would corner you," Jessie retorted.

"I didn't have to meet you again," Nadine barked back. "I could have just forgotten the whole thing."

"Will you two please be quiet?" Lawrence demanded. "You sound like an old married couple bickering over what to eat for dinner." The woman beside him let out a chuckle. "It wasn't meant to be funny, Veronica."

"Perhaps not," Veronica said, "but it was nonetheless. I have a feeling there is more to this story than we know. Nadine, why did you agree to meet with this boy again?"

"He had a box with an unusual design on it," Nadine confessed. "It was a Mermaid holding a large pearl. Jessie and his companions were trying to decipher the contents. I was curious as to what they were. I thought perhaps not everything was returned to the Mermaids as we previously had thought."

"Good gracious, child," Charles said. "Why didn't you come to me?"

"I was afraid the strangers would disappear if I alerted anyone," Nadine admitted. "They weren't alarmed by me. I figured if I could meet with them and take a look at the contents, I could figure out if we had a situation that warranted further investigation."

"Do you know how dangerous that was?" her father asked. "You could have been killed. We have no idea who these strangers are or what their purpose is."

"No, we don't," Lawrence interrupted. "What was in the box?"

"Clear map overlays and what looks like the notes of a pirate. It's all written in code that, at the time, I couldn't decipher."

"Thank you, Nadine," Veronica said. "You can sit down."

"Boy," Lawrence bellowed, "stand and state your name."

"Jessie."

"Well, Jessie," Lawrence said. "You have one chance to explain who you are, what you are doing with that box, and why you are here. Do you understand?"

"Yes," Jessie replied. He shifted his weight from one foot to the other, contemplating his words. "I'll save you the boring details. As a result of an attack on my people, my sister was inflicted with a serious illness - one that has caused her to age well beyond the norm for life in this realm. A friend of mine came across the box in question and a professor who claimed it held the secret to finding a mythical place called the Fountain of Youth. The water from this location is rumoured to be able to erase the effects of time. He claimed Mermaids were the key to finding it. Another friend of mine was present during the disturbance in the triangle. He was given a Merliance business card, in case he found out any information about the situation. We added everything up and found ourselves outside this complex."

"Young man," Veronica started, removing a pair of eyeglasses. "We have been guardians of the Mermaids since the beginning of time, during which never has there been any mention of the elusive Fountain of Youth. I think you may be barking up the wrong tree."

"With all due respect, Ma'am," Jessie replied. "My sister is in the condition she is in because she saved my life. I owe it to her to try."

"What you don't seem to understand," Lawrence explained, "is that we are responsible for the secrecy of an entire civilization."

"Then," Jessie replied, "Mermaids do exist?"

"Oh, they do exist," Lawrence answered. He leaned back, his chair squeaking under the pressure of his weight. He tossed his pen on the notepad in front of him. "Mermaids as a race don't bother with what we consider *our world* very much. In fact, it's centuries between sightings."

"We think of ourselves as liaisons, of sorts," Veronica continued. "Mermaids are delicate to deal with. A single cry from one can injure thousands in any realm. Together, their wailing could wipe out intelligent life. Acts of cruelty and destruction make them sad."

"If they have their own civilization away from us, why do they appear at all?" Jessie asked.

The Overseers exchanged glances. "Their existence relies on it," Veronica answered. "Like it or not, they cohabit here. What we do very much affects them. I do not believe they would permit the destruction of the land, through war or any other man-made act."

"So they come to check up on us?" Jessie questioned.

"There is another reason," Lawrence stated. "They need us to carry on their species."

"I'm not sure I follow," Jessie said.

"Mermaids," Veronica said, taking in an overly large breath of air, "are an entirely female race. While it is true they inhabit a place untouched by any other species, they still live much as anyone else with families and life partners."

"How do they reproduce?" Jessie asked, side-eyeing the Overseers. The answer wasn't something he was sure he wanted to know, but he felt compelled to hear out the rest of the story.

"They don't, often." Lawrence answered. "It's an unusual phenomenon for which we have no explanation. At intervals in history, a certain number of the colony swim to the surface. Along the way, they shed their tails and scales. They are left in a form similar to terunji women. Once on land, they find a suitable male and mate. After fertilization has taken place, they lay an egg. When the cycle is complete, their tail reforms and they return to the sea."

"What about breathing?" Jessie asked, trying to hide a forming frown.

"Mermaids have lungs as we do," Veronica explained. "They can breathe air anytime they want. The scales on their tail are what allow them to breathe underwater."

"What you are saying," Jessie commented, shaking his head, "is that you are basically an escort service for fish."

"It isn't that simple," Lawrence replied.

"What about the fathers?" Jessie interrupted. "Do they know about the half-breeds they are creating? Do they meet their children?"

"You are taking this out of proportion!" Lawrence yelled. "We ensure all mates are volunteers from within this compound. They know what they are agreeing to."

"The children don't become half-breeds," Veronica continued. "Only Mermaid genes are passed on. This is a better solution to having them look on their own for a mate.

We don't have to agree with the way things are. Nature would find a way to continue without us. Our way protects the other races that inhabit this world."

"So they simply disappear with these eggs?" Jessie asked, staring at the floor, his lips pressed tightly together.

"No, that is the other problem," Lawrence admitted. "The eggs have to be incubated above the water. They are very delicate and take centuries to come to full term."

"Are you saying you are an egg farm as well?"

"Goodness no," Lawrence answered. "The Mermaids have a place they protect with their own magicks where the eggs are kept. We know of only one group of pirates who made it to and off that island."

Jessie stumbled backwards, falling into a sitting position. "Pirates?" He asked. "You mean the pearl is a Mermaid egg?"

"Yes," Veronica answered. "We believe they were mistaken by pirates as large pearls and stolen. We also had thought they were all recovered. Nadine's great-grandparents were the ones to deliver them back to the Mermaid's Island. They haven't been heard from since. If eggs were missing when the Mermaids checked on them... well, you can imagine the tears that would follow. Nadine's great-grandmother is hailed a hero by our people."

"Then there is a chance that not all the eggs were recovered," Jessie said, rubbing his neck.

"If the documents you have are legitimate, and I believe from what Nadine has said they are, then we could have an apocalyptic-sized disaster looming over our heads," Lawrence admitted. "Where is the box now?"

"My two brothers and the Professor have gone in search of the pirate's buried treasure. They hope to retrieve the pearl and return it here."

"Well, that is good," Veronica said. "Hopefully they are successful in retrieving it, although I would have preferred to have some of our people along." She glanced at Nadine. "However, I think we understand why our young friend did what she did. It could have been a disaster if there is a pearl and it slipped through our fingers. Next time, let someone else in on the plan as well."

"Is that it?" Nadine squealed. "You aren't going to publicly punish me? I'm free to go?" Her beaming smile retreated as her eyes glanced over at the boy sitting beside her. "What about Jessie?"

"That," Veronica answered, "is a different story."

Jessie's head hung down, avoiding eye contact. Even if he made a run for it now, there was nowhere to go. Undoubtedly, the flaws in the security fence had been repaired overnight. If there was a way out, he couldn't think of it. His brows clenched together, protesting the dull ache that was beginning to grow in his temple.

"As you know," Lawrence continued, "we are burdened with the task of keeping the Mermaids and our organization a secret. No one is allowed to leave here without just cause and permission. This is an unusual case, as we have never had any one break in before." He held out one hand to collect pieces of paper from the rest of the Overseers. "It has been decided that Jessie shall remain in Merliance and join our forces."

"Remain for how long?" Jessie asked.

"For life," Veronica stated. "This isn't a fly-by-night operation. We take our roles here very seriously."

"If I find the answer to my sister's ailment..."

"If," Veronica interrupted, "such a cure exists and is found, we will find a way to convey it to those in a situation to help your sister. That is provided there are no consequences to ourselves or the Mermaids. In return, we ask you to agree to forfeit your life outside these walls. We will hold you to your word."

Jessie rubbed the back of his neck. For the first time, his gaze met the Overseers head-on. "I suppose I have no choice but to agree."

"No, you really don't," Lawrence replied, the corner of one side of his mouth curling upwards into a mocking smile.

"Then," Jessie said, taking in a breath of air, "I agree."

Chapter Thirteen

Pandora inhaled deeply. The next best thing to being in water was sailing on it. The gentle rock of the waves combined with the salty taste of the air relaxed every muscle. She closed her eyes, enjoying the sensation, only opening them to the splashes of the accompanying dolphins, travelling in the same direction.

"This is the life!" she yelled, extending both her arms wide. "Someone should learn how to bottle this feeling."

"I don't think the Professor shares your point of view," Dezi chuckled, nodding towards the man standing in the doorway to the under deck living quarters.

A mischievous smile graced Pandora's lips as she glanced over the greyish-coloured Professor. "Not found your sea legs yet?"

The Professor held onto the door frame with one hand. A life jacket struggled to contain his body within its protective hug. Noticeably absent was the box containing maps and notes, which had been left below. The tight hug that used to keep it safe now clung to a ring-shaped life preserver. He edged one foot onto the deck, moving cautiously as if the boat could collapse under his weight if he moved faster.

Pandora howled a laugh. "I've seen tightrope walkers move more quickly than you," she mocked.

"Can't we get there any faster?" Finkle complained.

"The boat can only go so fast, Professor," Pete answered from his station at the wheel. "I'm new to running one of these things too. There aren't any bodies of water in my home world."

"Yes, yes," the Professor barked. "I know all that. What I don't understand is why our Goddess isn't helping things along."

"Helping things along!" Pandora shrieked. "What am I supposed to do? I can't magically transport you to where you want to be."

"I had believed you to have some abilities at sea," Finkle complained. "Can't you hook those fish up and have them pull us faster?" He released the wooden pole he had stumbled into for a split second, just long enough to point in the direction of their dolphin escort.

"Hook them up?!" Pandora screamed. "You expect me to be cruel to these gentle creatures simply because of a bit of sea sickness? Preposterous! I wouldn't think of doing any such thing. Regardless, I doubt they would agree anyway."

"Am I to understand that you cannot control the sea life?" Finkle asked.

"I don't control any life other than my own," Pandora answered. "I can converse with them - I have even made friends with some, but that is the extent of the relationship between us."

"What bloody good is that?" Finkle asked, raising his voice a few octaves. "What exactly can our Goddess of the Sea do?"

"Do you really want to know?" An eerie chill accompanied Pandora's words as the fairly calm ocean began to stir. A shadowed smirk overtook her previous jovial appearance, the frightful manifestation of which was matched by the black pools forming in her eyes.

The dolphins took their leave, performing an acrobatic show as a goodbye. Waves crashed against the sides of the borrowed house boat, causing anything not nailed down on the deck to slide from side to side. The ocean misted down on them from each splash of the swelling sea. Massive crests formed accompanied by a white froth - the previously peaceful surface now rabid from Pandora's bite.

"Would a tsunami get you there fast enough?" Pandora giggled, pointing to the wall of water forming behind the tiny boat.

"Pandora!" Dezi yelled. "We need to live through this." He spat out salt water, his body now drenched.

Pandora turned her empty, blackened eyes to the boy hanging onto the side-railing for his life. She blinked twice, after which her pupils and the waters both calmed. The liquid wall which had been pursuing them, disappeared without a trace.

"My bad," Pandora said as an apology

Finkle fell to his knees, gasping for air. He crawled to the side of the boat, barely managing to pull himself up to the edge before vomit spewed out of his mouth. Even after his stomach was empty he continued to dry heave, his greyish colour not improving.

"Perhaps you should go inside until the ride is over," Pandora suggested. "Unless, of course, you'd like to pull out that wand of yours and show us if you have any magical abilities that could aid in the speed at which we reach our destination."

Finkle muttered his favourite choice words as he crawled his way back to the living quarters. "I may be at a disadvantage at sea," he whispered to himself, "but I am willing to bet I can best you on land, Pandora. We'll see who is laughing when this is all over." He plopped down on a chair and leaned back, trying to ignore the subtle rocking still stirring his stomach. A lopsided grin formed on his face as he imagined all the ways he could make a fool out of the woman he despised more than any other.

He sniffed in the remnants of salt water lingering in his nose, spitting it on the floor beside him. "Women are never worth the trouble they cause."

Chapter Fourteen

"Nadine!" Jessie called out. "Wait!" He hadn't seen her move that fast before. Keeping up without exposing his unusual abilities was a challenge, especially since he had no idea where he was going and would be lost without a guide.

"What?" Nadine answered, stopping abruptly.

"You could show me around a little," Jessie suggested. "I am new here and all. I don't have a clue where I am supposed to go, or what to do."

"This is home for you now," Nadine said, doing her best to brush him off. It was bound to happen sooner or later. He was the athletic, good-looking type who would fit in perfectly with the others. "You'll have no problem making new friends."

"What about you?" Jessie asked. "I thought we could be friends."

Nadine chuckled. "You'll fit in here well," she replied. "You don't need me holding you back." She started walking again.

Severing the ties now meant less pain later when she became forgettable.

"Can you show me around?" he pleaded.

Nadine shrugged her shoulders in defeat. The next half hour consisted of her pointing out the different buildings while trying to avoid eye contact. There was already enough heaviness in her heart, knowing soon he'd be one of them and she'd be alone again.

"This is the practice field," she said. "Danny, this is Jessie. He'll be joining the team from today on."

Danny extended a hand, surprising Jessie with a full body throw. "Nice to meet you," he said. "Around here, you need to be prepared for anything. This is where we learn that." He helped Jessie to his feet.

"Combat training or defence?" Jessie asked.

"A little of both," Danny explained. "Once you get a handle on things, the weapons are over here."

Jessie picked up a blade. Testing its sharpness, he sliced a cut in his finger. "Are they meant to be this dangerous? Don't schools usually use placeholders for weapons so no one is hurt?"

"What good is using a fake?" Danny replied. "Out there, if there is a battle, you'll be up against the real thing. This is the only way to make sure we are prepared. Don't worry, we have a good team of medics here that can save life or limb." He laughed.

"What makes you think I'm the one who will need saving?" Jessie's tone issued an undeniable challenge.

"Seems someone has some spunk," A blonde-haired girl called out from a growing crowd. "You going to let him talk to you like that?"

"Don't worry, Salem," Danny replied to her without taking his eyes off his new rival. "I'm going to give this outsider a warm welcome." He smiled. "That is, if you aren't afraid of a little skirmish."

Jessie chuckled. "Bring me what you got," he ordered. "I'm happy to put a guy like you in his place." His cocky attitude earned him a round of *oohs* and *ahs* from onlookers. He scanned their faces looking for a familiar one, but found only strangers. Frowning, he turned his attention back to his opponent already on the move.

He used only a portion of his speed to sidestep the attack. He twisted, landing a foot directly in the other boy's back. Danny fell to the ground, but didn't remain down, entering into a seamlessly-smooth kip up in the same motion.

"Not bad," Danny praised. "You have some speed, but you can't dodge every attack." He leapt forward, using a nearby trampoline to boost his height, coming down directly over-top of his target. His fist landed. "If there had been a weapon in my hand, you'd be dead right now."

"If you had a weapon in your hand, I might take you more seriously," Jessie barked back, rubbing his jaw from the impact. "Not a bad punch, but now it's my turn." A spilt second was all it took for Jessie to knock the strongest of their kind on his backside, seeing stars.

Danny never saw it coming. He shook his head, the metallic taste of blood fresh in his mouth. "That's quite the punch you pack."

Jessie sighed. "Sorry," he offered. "I didn't intend to hit you that hard." It was his turn to offer Danny a hand up.

"No," Danny smiled. "That's what training is about. We can never be prepared for the real thing if we are never challenged. It's good to have someone new to spar with around here." He offered his hand in friendship.

Jessie slapped his hand into a firm shake. "Thanks," he said. "Looks like this is my new home, so I hope I can get along with everyone."

"From what I just saw," Danny said, patting his new friend on the back, "you are going to fit right in. I can introduce you to the best-looking girls. Trust me, they'll swoon over a guy like you and I don't mind sharing."

"Thanks," Jessie replied, a bashful laugh escaping his lips. "There's really only one girl I'm interested in and I didn't see where she went."

"Oh yeah," Danny replied. "Which one?"

"Nadine," Jessie answered. "You didn't see which direction she went in, did you?"

"Nadine." Danny echoed. "Really? I'm not judging you for your taste, man, but there are some hot numbers living here I can hook you up with."

"Thanks for the offer," Jessie answered. "But I'm not interested. I really like Nadine."

Danny shook his head. "Okay, have it your way. I didn't see where she went, but I know where she is."

"Heads up!" someone in the distance yelled.

Danny swivelled to catch an incoming football. "You'll find her in the library. She's a disaster when it comes to anything athletic, but a whiz with the books."

"That's perfect," Jessie answered. "We can even each other out." He broke into a jog, heading towards the other side of the field. The library had been one of the first buildings on his earlier partial-tour. All he had left to do was convince Nadine they would work well together.

Chapter Fifteen

"Should we throw down an anchor?" Pete asked. The gentle hum of the engine ceased, leaving only the gentle splash of water to indicate they were still at sea.

"Here?" Pandora shrieked. "I thought we were hunting for buried treasure. Aren't we going to an island?"

"Not so much buried as submerged," Dezi replied. "The pirate map indicates it is located underwater right about here."

"Well," Pandora said, "then we have a very big problem."

"Problem?" Finkle said, emerging from below to investigate the silence of the engines. "Are we here?"

"We are," Dezi answered. "What's wrong with dropping anchor here?"

"What's wrong?" Pandora echoed, her voice raising slightly at the end. "This is the deepest part of the ocean. An anchor isn't going to reach."

"So don't throw one down," Finkle interrupted, one hand on his head. "Hurry up and go fetch the chest."

"Are you talking to me?" Pandora asked. "I'm not a dog."

"Oh, good gracious... here we go again," Finkle complained. "Yes, I am talking to you. You are the one who can turn into water and talk to fish."

"It's not that easy," Pandora argued.

"It never is," Finkle mumbled, shaking his head. The drooping skin on his cheeks vibrated with the motion.

"Must I explain the fundamentals of magic to you as well?" Pandora asked, her hands lodged on her hips.

Finkle plopped down on the deck. "I have a feeling we are going to be a while, might as well get comfortable." He motioned for the other two to join him.

"Here is the first problem," Pandora started, ignoring the Professor's antics. "The depth here is below what this flimsy body can withstand. That is why it remains the only undiscovered part of this world. This is where realms connect without the barriers that hinder life above the surface."

Finkle let out a huff of air. "Need I remind you that you can turn to water? As such, you need not worry about these inconsequential tribulations."

"For a professor," Pandora complained, "you aren't very bright. In liquid form, I can't grasp anything to bring it to the surface. Do you even know what the chest looks like? How heavy is it?"

"Just admit you aren't actually a Goddess and we will look for another way," Finkle blurted out.

"I didn't say I couldn't do it," Pandora retorted, a pout fully formed on plump lips. "There are considerations that need to be made, though."

"Like what?!" Finkle yelled.

"Like," Pandora barked back, "there are things that dwell deep beneath the surface that should never be disturbed. We could unleash something terrible into this world."

"I thought you could communicate with the creatures of the sea," Finkle snickered. "Not even a little?" His outstretched hand made a small gap between his thumb and index finger.

"Just because they can hear me, doesn't mean they listen," Pandora answered. "There are things even Gods should not meddle with."

"Are you afraid?"

"Yes, Professor," Pandora whispered. "And you should be too. If I go down and do this, I will be in no condition to help you should one of those creatures follow me back up."

"Why not?" the Professor questioned.

"The fundamentals of magic," Pandora answered, rolling her eyes. "It takes a large amount of energy to perform the tasks you are asking me to. My power will be exhausted upon return."

"We'll worry about that when the time comes," the Professor replied, a shaky smile trying to take form as he spoke.

"Why would pirates hide something where they couldn't retrieve it?" Dezi asked. "It seems rather silly."

"They might not have realized that the sea floor was so far down here," Pandora answered. "If they were being chased, they might have thrown it overboard, planning to come back later. To be honest, most treasures of this type have been found. The only reason this one might still exist is because of where it rests. It is both a good and bad thing for our quest."

"Maybe we should put a little more thought into this," Pete offered. "Plan it a little better."

"Do you want to save your sister?" the Professor snapped. "We can't help her without that pearl."

Before another word could be uttered, Pandora dove into the ocean - a flawless entrance, barely disturbing the natural ripples of the surface.

"I guess that settles things!" Finkle exclaimed, clapping his hands together. "What shall we do while we wait?" An escaping chuckle mutated into an unsettling laugh that sounded as devious as the contents of his mind.

"I suggest we prepare for the unexpected," Pete replied. "I have a bad feeling things aren't going to go as smoothly as the trip over."

Finkle gulped back a mouthful of saliva, reminding him of the episode Pandora had caused earlier. If he played his cards right, he could pay her back while still at sea. A menacing gurgling noise escaped his throat at the thought of the witch being too tired to defend herself after completing her task. He masked both the noise and his grin, leaning over the rail, using another bout of seasickness as a costume.

Chapter Sixteen

Jessie couldn't help but grin. Everything about Nadine made him feel warm inside. In his eyes, she was the definition of beautiful. Standing there watching had been easy until a pencil pushed against her cheek, pulling her hair back, before resting behind one ear. If only it had been his fingers that grazed over her smooth, dark skin, tidying back the stray curls.

"Are you going to stand there and watch me all day?" Nadine complained. "It's a little creepy."

"Sorry," Jessie muttered, a red flush creeping over his face. "I didn't want to disturb your concentration."

"What are you doing here?" Nadine asked. "I introduced you to Danny. You fit in better out there than in here."

"That's not fair," Jessie argued. "Maybe I enjoy books and things."

"Uh-huh," Nadine said, arching her eyebrows without looking up. "Books and... things." She shook her head, refusing to be caught up in a game of cat and mouse. She already knew as the mouse she'd be teased and toyed with, possibly injured and left for dead on her parents' doorstep.

"Besides," Jessie started, "I am not going to find a cure for my sister out there. In here is the only place that could hold an answer. I need your help."

Nadine bit her top lip. Glancing up, her gaze met his. That was a mistake. A warmness surrounded her with all the power of the sun's rays on the hottest summer day. This stranger somehow made her feel more special than even her closest relatives ever had. But why?

"Fine," she mumbled, swallowing as many emotions as she could. Vulnerable was one term no one would ever use to describe her.

"Thank you," Jessie replied, moving the seat next to her closer. "Where do we start? Is there a certain book I should read?"

Nadine couldn't help but smile at the enthusiasm dripping off his words. This was a new side to him - one she hadn't noticed before and, unfortunately, it made him twice as attractive. Being able to ask for help wasn't something a large percentage of the male population in Merliance was capable of.

"I know!" Jessie exclaimed, his eyes widening with his smile. He stood, shoving one hand in his pocket. When it emerged again, papers came along with it. "You could take a look at the notes. Maybe you can figure out how to break the code they are written in."

"You brought them?!" Nadine screamed, earning her a few grumbles from the library staff.

"They are actually just copies," Jessie admitted. "I hope that doesn't make a difference. I figured they would come in handy."

"You figured right," Nadine answered, her aura glowing. "It will probably take me a few days to break their code." Her eyes scanned the papers, taking in all the letters and symbols. "Did you happen to bring a copy of the maps as well?"

"Yeah," Jessie answered, tossing the clear sheets on the table. "Do you think they will figure in?"

"I don't know," Nadine mumbled. "But I don't want to overlook anything. I have a feeling that the notes are a retelling of the way in and out of a Mermaid sanctuary where their eggs are kept."

"You don't know where it is?" Jessie asked, arching an eyebrow.

"We know where it is," Nadine explained, "but not how the pirates got in and out of all the wards and spells in place."

"How did your great-grandmother do it?" Jessie asked.

"I don't know," Nadine replied. "It was a one way trip for her. I don't believe she ever expected to return."

"How do you know she made it?" Jessie questioned.

"I suppose we don't," Nadine replied. "We always assumed that she was successful because... well, we are still here. If the eggs were discovered missing and the Mermaids cried, life as we know it would be wiped out."

"I hate to be negative," Jessie commented, "but if an egg is missing, isn't it possible that the Mermaids haven't figured it out yet?"

Nadine dropped her pencil. Her head slowly turned to face Jessie's. "I never thought of that," she admitted. "We could have a much bigger issue to handle than we thought. If your theory is correct, potentially we are fighting against a doomsday clock that has been silently ticking for a very long time."

"I suppose the only way to stop it is to return the pearl?" Jessie asked. "Guess that's in my brothers' hands now."

"Let's hope they can find it and get back here before our time is up," Nadine said. "For now, we can only put efforts into finding a way to return the egg to its rightful place safely."

"What can I do?" Jessie asked.

"Let's start with finding books to do with pirate terms and their meanings," Nadine answered. "We'll also need anything that references symbols that might have been used. If we replace all of them in these pages, we might be able to fill in the rest."

Chapter Seventeen

The swim down was the easy part. In her liquid form, Pandora could move easily and quickly, descending to points others only dreamed existed - neither the frigid temperature nor the pressure able to affect her.

A colourful school of fish swam by in a diamond formation. Pandora flipped to move out of their way. Even made of liquid, she still occupied space. Her very existence in this habitat could disrupt the delicate ecosystem. That was something the marine life had enough of in this world without her adding to it. Had she not been made out of and surrounded by liquid, a tear might have shed for the recent sights of majestic creatures beaching themselves amidst disorientation.

The further she descended, the darker it became. Her magic adjusted her sight to accommodate, however some shadows still remained. These darker spots were the unknown factor that could cause ruin to her mission. Depth held no meaning here. Rocks appearing within grasp could take hours to reach. That was life under the ocean's surface - not meant for land dwellers to ever experience.

The danger factor played its hand amongst a peachy coral reef, riddled with pink nodules - the perfect hiding spot for predators to lie in wait. One never knew what could be lurking around the corner. If she was lucky, the treasure would be in the open and easy to locate. If not, she would have to chance disturbing creatures slumbering in coral caves, some of whom wouldn't take to kindly to being woken up.

Pandora pushed further into the deep. Her life force extending into limbs, the two back legs moving similar to a fish's tail and her arms outstretched, exploring every surface spot they could find. If she had been in flesh form, the jagged edges of recently broken coral would have easily sliced through her skin. Although it would be only a superficial wound, the resulting blood would have called every predator in the area directly to her. The way back up needed a whole lot more caution on her part.

Pandora spun around, knocked off her direction by a rather large ugly fish. It wasn't a species she had met before and apparently it either didn't or couldn't see her subtle outline. Despite its size, it swam away, frightened by the unexpected collision. Again, she had been lucky she wasn't in her body form or that encounter most likely would have gone in a totally different direction. It was only the element of surprise that drove the sea beast away.

The effects of continuous magic use would start to take its toll soon. It was impossible to tell how long she had been submerged or even how far down she had travelled. She needed as much energy as possible for the trip back - that meant conservation was the name of the game. This wasn't the same as diving in and swimming with dolphins. The further down she went, the less chance of successfully returning to the top. Pandora would never admit it to the others, but not even she had ever found the absolute bottom - if there was one.

A gut feeling made her swerve towards a series of caverns in which the openings were big enough to manoeuvre. The naturally-formed structure rivalled some of the finest architecture seen above ground. A series of twists and turns formed a maze, which, when followed correctly, led to an amphitheatre-sized midsection. There in the middle of the circular room was an old chest, partially buried in the sand.

As much as locating the chest was an exhilarating feeling, it also brought about a sense of impending doom. Moving to it in her current form unnoticed was easy. Leaving was going to be another story. This was a breeding ground she didn't want to be caught in. The chest itself could have very well been a child's toy. Taking candy from a baby might be easy for land dwellers, but taking something away from even the smallest giant squid was another.

She surveyed the area and pondered her options. There was no sign of any parents, but at least a half a dozen babies to deal with. There was little choice but to try to move the chest in her current form, at least outside the maze. Hopefully, it wouldn't upset any of the little ones to see it leave.

Vines of sea plants crept passed her, wrapping around the pirate's stash. She backed up slowly, using the plants to drag the treasure beside her. Inch by inch, she weaved her way through outstretched tentacles, making sure not to disturb a single resting child.

The effects of prolonged exposure to the depth began to weaken her magic. She was tiring from exerting energy. A momentary lapse in judgement meant taking a wrong turn in the labyrinth that stood between her and a clear path to the surface world. Backtracking added valuable time onto her mission. She cursed herself for agreeing to the job in the first place. When the exit appeared on her scope, excitement overtook caution. Like a bullet, she sped to the opening, almost colliding with the back of one of the young squid. Pandora darted back behind the wall. This baby sea creature was larger than any recorded squid known and it was searching for something.

Pandora glanced back at the chest. Her first instinct had been correct. This treasure was as valuable to this youngster as it was to her friends. Getting it to the surface without being followed was going to be even harder than expected. For now, she'd have to wait and hope for an opportunity to arise. As if reading her thoughts, the baby darted off to the left and out of sight. It probably hadn't gone far, but Pandora needed to take advantage of the situation.

The vines of sea plants hurled the chest upwards. Pandora swam after it, changing into a solid form in time to grab both sides. The weight pulled her down, something she hadn't anticipated. Adding additional magic into the fray, Pandora put everything into the upwards climb. She could feel her strength begin to falter as reflections of light appeared. Adrenaline fuelled a final push as the bottom of the boat came into view. Only a few minutes more and she'd be on the surface again. She'd made it.

Glancing back over her shoulder, an object came into view. She panicked, flailing as she burst through to fresh air.

"Take this!" Pandora screamed.

Pete grabbed the chest and heaved it onto the deck. Dezi did the same with Pandora's limp body.

"Go fast!" Pandora commanded before collapsing.

Chapter Eighteen

Pandora gasped for air. She hadn't felt this worn out since the fight with Cornost in the Elf realm. Her head tilted towards the chest lying beside her. The task was complete, but would they survive to see the rest of the quest to its completion?

Pandora caught sight of the Professor emerging from the deck below. The sinister glimmer in his eye and wand in his hand meant trouble. He lingered in the doorway, a worrisome grin taking form from the corners of his lips.

The boat lunged forward, engines on full. The Professor's body jerked, but remained sturdy, using the door frame for support. The seasickness which had stricken the man on the voyage there had all but disappeared - replaced by a motivation which reeked of revenge. Pandora felt mal intent surrounding her as the Professor edged forward in her direction. Unsure whether it was real or an overactive imagination, she saw her life pass by, all reflected in the dark centres of Finkle's eyes.

The Professor froze. His expression morphed. What was once something to be feared was now the one afraid.

Pandora searched for the meaning of his transformation, still too weak to move. Finkle's pupils dilated, no longer reflecting back shadows of her life, but rather the image of an oncoming attack - tentacles reaching up out of the sea.

The vessel shook, from the weight of two large squid arms coming down on the backside, raising the front to heights a boat should never achieve. Finkle backtracked to the doorway, falling to his knees. His grip latched on to the sturdiest part of the ship he could find.

There was nothing for Pandora to hold onto. Her limp body slid along with the chest. She muffled a cry, too proud to allow anyone to see her cower.

"Professor!" Pete yelled, "take the wheel!" Without waiting for an answer, he slid towards the back of the ship. "Dezi, I can't put up a barrier until the tentacles release us."

"On it," Dezi replied. "I'll give it a good taste of voltage. That should make it let go. Be ready to put up the shield."

Pandora crawled her way back up the deck, using fingernails and adrenaline to fuel her efforts. She glanced over at the Professor still sitting in the same position, his eyes clenched as tight as his grip around his wand. There was no choice but to make it to the wheel. Someone had to take control once they were free. She pulled herself up to a standing position and held on tight, awaiting her cue.

A bolt of energy surged from Dezi's fingertips. The baby squid, rather than letting go, gripped stronger, threatening to tear the boat apart.

"It didn't work!" Pete yelled, turning his attention to stopping water from flooding the deck. "Try again."

Dezi nodded. He dug deep inside and pulled out every bit of magic he could muster. This was their final chance. A bolt of energy flew through the air, hitting their attacker dead-centre. The squid flew backwards, landing with a splash almost as big as the one their own boat made, falling back down onto the surface. Pete immediately encased the area with a shield to prevent a second attack. The boat puttered forward, the motor damaged.

Dezi took over the helm. Pandora fell back down, slumping into a sitting position, propped up by the ship's frame.

"It's on the move again!" Pete exclaimed. "I don't know how long I can hold the shield in place."

"I gave everything in that last burst of power," Dezi commented. "I won't be able to muster up that sort of strength again right away."

"Professor!" Pete yelled. "Use your wand. From here, you have a clear shot."

"I'm a potion master!" the Professor exclaimed. "I don't have any spells for getting rid of a giant squid. Ask your Sea Goddess! Where is her magic?"

"She's still wiped out from retrieving the chest," Dezi replied. "She can barely move. We need your help!"

"Barely move?" the Professor questioned. "Am I to believe that the Pandora of legends is that weak? How did she ever manage to go down in history as the owner of a box that could bring about the apocalypse? Well, Pandora, where are your horsemen now?"

Pandora held one arm against her midsection. She fell slightly to the right, sitting lopsided, still requiring the side of the boat to prop her up. The corners of her mouth gently curled up. "You are right, Professor. Thank you for reminding me." With her free hand, she produced a small glowing box. The lid sprung open making way four ghostly figures of men on steeds.

Dezi's eyes widened. "Are they..."

"My faithful friends," Pandora began, ignoring everything around her, "I have a favour to ask. This is not the normal task I ask of you. I need you to harness to the front of the ship and use your strength to pull it with speed."

The ghostly figures glanced at each other and then back at Pandora without moving. Their expressions, while dark and unnerving, held a dash of confusion. This wasn't what they had been created for. Their purpose was chaos, destruction, war. They were meant to end a battle just begun - not to tow a broken boat to shore.

Pandora took in a breath of deep air. "I promise you, my friends, a battle is brewing and one in which you will be able to unleash your terror. If you are to see that day, I must see another."

The horsemen nodded, satisfied with their mistress' explanation. They took flight to the water's surface, a ghostly harness appeared, latching onto the front of the ship. With the speed of the wind, the vessel raced away from the pursuing squid.

"I thought you were out of power," Pete said, taking a seat beside Pandora. "Don't get me wrong, I'm glad you aren't."

Pandora chuckled. "They are my familiars. I don't need to support them with energy. They aren't used to being asked to do manual labour, but it was worth a shot. I guess Finkle was useful for something... coming up with the idea."

Pete laughed. "Should we tell him it's safe?"

"No," Pandora said. "Let me regain a bit of strength first. I don't trust that man. I have a feeling if that baby hadn't attacked us, he would have finished me off back there on the deck."

"Wait!" Dezi exclaimed. "You mean that squid was only a baby?"

"Yes," Pandora answered. "Let's hope it doesn't go crying back to mommy. If she shows up, we are in a world of trouble."

"Why did it attack us?" Pete asked.

"The chest," Pandora answered. "I believe it is similar to a security blanket. My guess is it gives off a comforting feeling."

"No!" the Professor screamed, kneeling beside the chest.

"What's with him?" Pete asked.

"He just figured out the chest is sealed air tight," Pandora chuckled. "There is a specific way it has to be opened."

"That's probably what the notes are about," Pete suggested.

"Hopefully, your brother found a way to decipher them," Pandora said. "I'd hate to think we went through all this and couldn't open it."

Chapter Nineteen

"It's starting to make sense!" Nadine exclaimed. She glanced around, hoping the librarians hadn't heard her outburst.

"Don't worry. They aren't here," Jessie said, his head resting on top of a book. "I think the library closed an hour ago."

"Oh," Nadine replied. "Well, I think I understand how to read this. I've replaced all the known pirate terms with what we believe them to mean and it looks like a story in diary form. There are a few pages missing."

Jessie pushed himself to a sitting position, a wobbly one, but sitting nonetheless. His brows arched, forcing his eyelids to open. It was late - too late. The two of them should have called it an evening when the library staff left. He glanced over at Nadine, wondering how she continued reading when he could barely focus. He opened his mouth to speak, but a yawn took the place of words. His hand raced to cover the opening, finding something even worse than an open mouth.

Slobber crust had formed on the left side of his chin. He wiped it away, turning the action into a stretch to cover up.

"This is amazing," Nadine said, ignoring his movements. "It appears that the leader of our pirates met a competing captain in a house of ill repute. After a night of drinking, things turned physical. They not only defeated the other pirates, but took their ship and the other captain was murdered."

"Sounds like a tall tale," Jessie said, his posture sinking back towards using the table as a pillow.

"It gets better," Nadine replied. "The leader of the pirates we are interested in ripped the heart out of the other captain while he was still standing. The new boat was an upgrade so they took it over. Inside the captain's quarters was a chest. Not an ordinary chest - a magic one. They tortured the first mate until they learnt the secret to opening it."

Jessie's head lifted up. "This is a rather gruesome bedtime story."

"It doesn't end there," Nadine explained. "You'll never guess the rest."

"They decided to keep the old captain's heart inside the chest, still beating?" Jessie asked.

"No," Nadine answered, scrunching up her nose. "Why would he do that? Actually, he threw the heart overboard to attract sharks for when he made the rest of the old crew walk the plank."

"That's rather horrifying," Jessie said, a lump forming in his throat. Dying was one thing, but being eaten alive was another.

"That's not where I was going with the story, though," Nadine said, her words getting faster. "They found out you have to pour alcohol over top of the chest and set it on fire.

When the flames die down, it leaves a mark in which a single drop of the original captain's blood has to be placed."

"Okay," Jessie said. "Except he's dead. How are we supposed to open it without his blood?"

"I was getting to that," Nadine answered. "Inside the large chest, the new captain found a smaller box - one with a diagram of a Mermaid on it holding a pearl."

"The box the Professor is carrying," Jessie mumbled.

"Get this," Nadine said, nodding. "There is a hidden compartment inside that box where the pirates stashed a vial of the blood needed to open the larger chest, as well as maps to a hidden Island."

"So we need to take another look at that box!" Jessie exclaimed. "But, how did they get maps to the Mermaids if no one knew they existed?"

"It gets a little hard to decipher from there," Nadine admitted. "There are pages missing. I am hoping we find them in the secret compartment as well. From what I gather, the dead crew weren't the thieves. They won the chest with one pearl inside already in a game of chance."

"That's why your great-grandparents didn't know it was missing. They recovered all the others and returned them," Jessie said, leaning his chair back on two legs. A single crack was all it took to send him to the ground amidst broken pieces of wood.

"Yes," Nadine smirked. "I should have mentioned you shouldn't lean back too far in these seats. They aren't in the best shape."

"Thanks," Jessie huffed, pulling himself up.

"It seems our pirates took care of things after learning of the fate of the other crew. They stashed the chest in a safe place, keeping out the smaller box," Nadine continued. "They probably planned to go back later when things cooled down."

"So, why didn't they?" Jessie asked.

"Not sure," Nadine answered. "Like I said, pages are missing. There is, however, mention of something that will interest you."

"What?" Jessie asked, frustrated at her pause.

"They left inside the treasure chest the pearl and a knife," Nadine answered. "The only weapon known to be able to release a liquid that is thought to make one live forever."

"The Fountain of Youth!" Jessie exclaimed.

"It sounds like it," Nadine answered. "We may be able to save your sister, after all. That's all I can get from these papers."

"That's enough to go on," Jessie said. "Now we wait for my brothers to return - hopefully with more answers."

Chapter Twenty

"There's a woman in the river asking for you," Lawrence said.

"A woman?" Jessie replied, still half-asleep.

"She appeared out of the water," Lawrence commented, sitting on the edge of the bed. "I hear it was quite the show."

"That would be Pandora," Jessie explained.

"Pandora," the Overseer repeated, one eyebrow arching high above the other. "As in Pandora's box?"

Jessie sighed. He rubbed the crusted corners of his eyes removing all traces of the sandman's handiwork. "I think so," he answered, pulling himself to a sitting position. He had been reading books well into the time he needed for sleep - both eyes confirmed that, refusing to open fully. "She prefers to be referred to as the Goddess of the Sea."

"What is she doing here?" Lawrence asked.

"Looking for me," Jessie answered. "My brothers must be back with the pearl. I might have forgotten to mention her before."

"Yes," Lawrence replied, arching the other eyebrow, "I believe you did. Is there anything else we should know?"

"I wouldn't make her angry," Jessie replied. "She dances to her own tune, if you know what I mean." He pulled on a pair of track pants and a shirt. "Where is she now?"

"Still down by the river bank," Lawrence answered. "We weren't sure what to make of her. One of the guards said she materialized out of water. I'm sure you can understand our concern about how many people seem to know about our secret organization."

"I'd suggest you stop giving out business cards then," Jessie joked. "That's what brought us here. If you are worried about Pandora, don't be. She lays claim to being the reason behind most of the historically recorded Mermaid sightings. You might actually enjoy chatting with her. Don't expect her to agree to stick around, though. I doubt you have anything that could contain her."

"Wonderful," Lawrence replied, rolling his eyes. "Shall we go meet this Goddess?"

Discussing everything that had happened in front of one of the Overseers wasn't the way Jessie had hoped to make contact with the others, but it would have to do. Options for communicating outside the security fence were limited. What they had once considered a way to keep strangers out now seemed more likely a tool to keep the Merliance population locked in.

As they walked over the ridge, Jessie looked down, realizing he wasn't wearing shoes. The cool dew forming a sheer sheet over blue grass soaked the bottom of his pants, sending shivers up his legs as messengers with an unpleasant reminder of the consequences of his forgetfulness.

The rays of a full moon glowed glory down on Pandora, her bare feet being tickled by the river dancing under them. She fired off regal glances, darting between each of the gathered spectators - daring them to make the wrong move.

"You look a bit tired," Jessie said.

"Good to see you too," Pandora called out. "It was a long journey, but we have returned. What about you? Is everything okay here?"

"I've joined Merliance," Jessie blurted out.

"I'm sorry?" Pandora said, her voice lifting to make a question. "You did what? I would have thought that serious a decision should have been a group thing."

"I'm working with them," Jessie explained. "Is everyone alright from the trip? I trust it was successful?"

"Yes," Pandora said, side-eyeing the guards inching closer. "We are all fine. The mission was a success with only a few minor hiccups." She shifted her stance. "What's really going on here?"

"The people who run Merliance would like a few words in private," Jessie replied. "They aren't accustomed to having visitors."

Pandora laughed. "If they want to speak to me in private, they need only send all these spectators away. I am happy to parley." She flashed a wicked grin, the pupils of her eyes expanding.

Jessie took a step back. "I suggest you talk to her here. She isn't one for taking orders. Her terms are usually the ones everyone goes by."

Lawrence flashed a glare of disapproval before letting out a huff. "Very well." He motioned with two fingers for the guards and spectators to clear the area.

"That's better," Pandora said, making her way to the edge of the water. Toes pointed like a dancer, her foot made contact with the wet grass - the dew cushioning her steps much in the same way the river had previously. "So, what's this all about?"

Jessie bit his bottom lip hoping the Overseer would take over the conversation. It took less than a minute to realize that wasn't going to happen. "The leaders of Merliance are not accustomed to allowing strangers inside." He paused for a moment, looking for the right words. "They are afraid their secret has been compromised. I agreed to remain a member of this society as proof I am not a threat."

"I see," Pandora said. "And I suppose they want all of us to join up in their little cult? Sorry, but I don't think so." She placed both hands on her hips, daring anyone to challenge her.

"It is for your own safety as well," Lawrence interrupted.

Jessie took another step backwards, cringing from the words. "He isn't familiar with who you are, Pandora..."

"My safety," Pandora repeated, the black of her pupils now filling both eyes. One side of her upper lip raised, the edges of the other curling. She raised her arms commanding a wall of water to rise behind her - drying the river. "Does it look like I need your protection?"

"Goddess," Jessie whispered to the Overseer out of a small crack in closed lips. He motioned with his eyes for the man to move forward.

Lawrence took the hint, edging closer. "My Lady," he said, his arms in the air, palms forward. "I didn't mean to upset you." He glanced at Jessie for approval before continuing. "Of course, a Goddess such as yourself should have the opportunity to come and go as you please."

Pandora eyed the man up and down. "Go on." The water returned to its rightful place in the river.

"The boy is young and inexperienced," Lawrence stated. "We have cause to worry about our secret being revealed. We need some assurances."

"I am willing to stay," Jessie said. "That was my choice. In doing so, I hope the good people in charge will allow my brothers to remain free. They will hardly divulge secrets that could bring harm to a family member."

"If what was stolen is returned," Lawrence said. "I believe we can make some sort of arrangement along those terms. Am I to understand you have the Pearl?"

"We have the chest," Pandora answered.

"They won't know how to open it..." Jessie began.

"Yes," Lawrence said, motioning for him to remain silent. "I read Nadine's report before I came for you."

"She stayed up and wrote a report?" Jessie asked, his brows raising. "I don't know how she does it. I was so tired."

"Bring us the chest," Lawrence demanded.

Pandora alternated glances between the two. "No, I don't think so. We are part of whatever is happening."

"That pearl belongs to the Mermaids," Lawrence stated. "We need to return it to them rather quickly."

Pandora opened her mouth to speak, but remained silent, seeing Jessie's finger raise in the air.

"The Pearl is a fertilized egg," Jessie explained. "It needs to be returned before its mother finds out it is missing."

Lawrence threw his hands in the air and smacked them back down against his sides. "What don't you understand about secret? This is exactly why we can't trust you to leave." He shook his head.

"Sir," Jessie relied. "I don't think you fully realize who Pandora is. She is most of your unexplained Mermaid sightings. I was browsing through books last night. Her knowledge alone could fill in generations of gaps in information."

Lawrence shifted his weight between legs, alternating glances between the two. "You're serious?"

"Quite," Pandora answered, patting the sides of her hair. "I know more about the oceans than fish do."

"If the trip to return the pearl is as difficult as Nadine suggests, we will need Pandora's help to make it." Jessie ran his hand through his hair. He was running out of convincing things to say.

"Okay, let's say I agree with that," Lawrence said, looking down at his shoes. "How do we know you won't skip off somewhere?"

"We work together," Jessie suggested. "You send some of your people to join us. If none of us return, you don't need to worry about your secret getting out anymore either. It's a win for you."

Lawrence pursed his lips together, his brows bunching together into one. "Agreed!" he exclaimed, raising one finger. "As long as there is an egg to return. We still don't know what is in the chest."

"The notes do make it clear," Jessie replied.

"Yes," Lawrence said. "They also are missing pages and incomplete. I want proof that the trip needs to be made."

"Pandora," Jessie said. "Do you still have the box? The one the maps were in."

"I believe so," Pandora answered. "The Professor lost interest in it after the treasure chest appeared. I'm sure one of you brothers grabbed it, though."

"We need to examine it again," Jessie explained. He turned to the Overseer. "If the box has the items Nadine said it does, we should leave immediately. Send a team to meet my brothers so we can open it and check. If the pearl is there, we'll set sail right away. If not, I'll return with your people. I ask my brothers be able to search elsewhere for a cure for my sister."

"Agreed!" Lawrence announced. "I'll have a team ready in thirty minutes. You can leave by the gate." He motioned towards Pandora.

Pandora smiled. "Thanks," she said, firing off a wink. "I prefer my way." Her skin shimmered, turning to clear liquid before spouting backwards into the river and disappearing.

"That's something you don't see every day," Lawrence muttered, shaking his head. He slapped Jessie on the back.

"In my world, you do," Jessie replied. "This place is rather calm in comparison. I might like taking it easy."

"Don't get too comfortable," Lawrence laughed. "The journey is just beginning."

Chapter Twenty-One

Pete was happy to give up his station at the wheel to a more experienced sailor. Merliance had provided a much bigger vessel for them to use, one which he wasn't comfortable manoeuvring. The last trip had been his first attempt at operating a boat. While he felt he did an okay job, his inexperience could hamper their voyage, especially if the trip was going to be as tough as was claimed.

Descending stairs, Pete joined the others below deck. Stuffed into a small living space, the others huddled around poking and prodding, each trying to piece together the growing puzzle. The box flipped over more than a dozen times. They knocked on the outside, then the inside.

"What, exactly, are we looking for?" Finkle asked. "We have been over every inch of the inside of the box ample times. There's nothing there."

"No," Nadine answered. "There isn't." She rubbed the dull ache growing in her temples. It had started the moment her foot touched the deck of the boat. Now, it grew with every word Finkle spoke. His voice irritated her in ways she didn't know were possible. As much as she tried, she couldn't push out of her mind a nagging feeling he was up to no good. This time, however, his words ran true. There simply wasn't anything inside the box. "Inside the box," she muttered, her eyes widening to match her growing excitement.

"What?" Finkle asked, directing a frown at the girl genius.

"I said... inside the box." Nadine flipped the cover closed. Her fingers traced the three-dimensional pictures, lingering on the pearl. A half-grin graced her lips, allowing a soft chuckle to escape. "Of course," she said, her eyes widening. "A secret."

"Perhaps you could share your thoughts with those of us who don't have the same enlightenment into the situation?" Finkle complained.

"The pearl is a Mermaid's secret," Nadine replied without looking away from the box. "It makes sense there would be something hidden inside. I need sea water!"

"Sea water - what in the realms for?" Finkle asked, tapping his foot.

Jessie handed a cup to Nadine. She glanced at him twice. If he hadn't had the water, she wouldn't have known he moved. "Thanks," she muttered, eyeing him carefully. "That was quick." She thought back to the breeze that passed her going through the security fence and understood. Jessie, with everything else as perfect about him as it was, also had the gift of speed.

"What do you need water for?" Finkle asked.

"Mermaids keep the... pearls above sea level," Nadine answered. "They never touch the ocean. I'm betting water opens a secret compartment."

"That's absurd," Finkle complained. "The chest was found at the bottom of the ocean - under the water. There is a pearl in there."

"Yes," Pete replied. "But the chest has an airtight seal. No water would get in. Regardless, we aren't worried about the chest right now, just the box. Give it a try. I think you may be on to something."

Nadine poured the liquid over top of the depiction of the pearl, making sure every part received an equal soaking. She jumped back, worried they had moved on impulse rather thinking the situation through.

"Nothing!" Finkle complained.

"Shh!" Pandora commented "Do you hear that?"

A gnawing sound similar to rodents inside a wall became louder. The upper half of the pearl began to move, turning clockwise. It halted, changing direction. Two turns later, the top popped off, revealing an array of items.

Finkle's eyes widened. "That's it!" He lunged forward, bouncing back off of Jessie's chest. "Move, you big goat!"

"Relax," Jessie said. "Let Nadine examine it first."

"Let her examine it?!" the Professor shrieked. "It's my box! The contents belong to me. This is my life's work and I demand to have a chance to look at it."

Rummaging through the compartment, Nadine palmed a vial of dark liquid. "It's okay," Nadine said, taking a step back. "The more people going over the maps, the better. We need to set course for Mermaid Isle immediately." She nodded at Jessie to move away.

"I see you've become this girl's hired help," Finkle scoffed. "You need to remember the advice I gave you. Nothing good will come from acting like a lost puppy. You are nothing more than hired muscle." He pushed by to the papers, already spilled out on the table.

While the others began pouring over maps and charts for the best route to take, Nadine and Jessie began their own investigation. Opening the chest in front of Finkle would no doubt prove disastrous.

Nadine plopped on a chair, expecting to sink, but finding it hard instead. Her lips curled downwards as she rubbed the area above her tailbone. The accommodations were nice for a life on the ocean, but she wasn't what one would call a typical sea dweller. A huff of air escaped her growing frown.

"Take your mind off it for a bit," Jessie suggested. "Let's check out the galley. Maybe we can find something to make for dinner."

"Okay," she agreed, her hand accepting the one he had offered. Their grips tightened, his strength pulling her up. The force was more than she expected, her feet tangled together, sending her face-first into his chest. His arms wrapped around her, holding her safe from a fall.

"Are you alright?" Jessie asked. "Sometimes I don't know my own strength."

"Yeah," she answered, gazing up. The warmth radiating from his eyes enveloped her, a blush creeping into her cheeks. "Sorry," she muttered, pushing away. "I can be a bit of a klutz sometimes."

"Sometimes," Danny echoed. "That's an understatement." He winked at Nadine, a smile forming from the colour taking over her face. "I wanted to make sure you two heard. They found a route to take, so we are about to push off."

"Great," Jessie replied. "We're headed to fix something for dinner. We'll have a plate brought up to you when it's done."

"Good stuff," Danny answered, his toothy smile glaring. "Jax and I are going to take turns navigating. There aren't enough rooms down here for everyone. Some of us will need to sleep up top under the stars."

"That's fine by me. I'd be happy to offer to take one of those spots," Jessie said. "I like the fresh air."

Nadine shook her head. "Let's go, big guy," she ordered, heading to the kitchen. She'd thought they were on the same wavelength, but in reality, Jessie had no idea what she was thinking. She needed him downstairs to try to open the chest later, not swooning under the stars. Although if the circumstances had been different, she might have enjoyed a night in his arms under the moonlight.

Nadine had never had an imagination worth speaking of and she cursed under her breath at it not only making a debut appearance now, but working overtime to boot. She blinked, trying to remove images of Jessie from her mind. She sighed. His being right next to her wasn't helping.

Chapter Twenty-Two

Nadine poked Jessie's arm. He snorted, doing little other than swatting her hand away. She paused, enjoying the way the light of the moon was shining down on him as he slept on the deck. She tapped him again, this time a bit harder. His muscles flexed, taking her breath away. He was almost perfect - trust was the only thing standing in the way. That was something that needed to be earned. She'd heard the others whisper about his interest in her - a part of her even wanted to believe it. While he had a personal agenda, she couldn't.

Jessie opened one eye just wider than a slit. "Hey," he whispered, his voice dry and gruff.

"Come on," she said, motioning for him to move.

"Now?" he complained. The movement of the waves urged him to fall back down - offering him a gentle rocking that guaranteed a deep and satisfying slumber. Fresh sea air filled his lungs, reminding him of a lazy day relaxing in a tree in his homeland - a light breeze gently fanning away the heat.

"Shh," she said, a finger over her puckered lips. She tiptoed back to the stairs leading to living quarters below.

Jessie shook the pleasant visions left over from his slumber from his thoughts. The past was a closed chapter in his life for a reason. The girl trying desperately not to tumble, making her way across the deck, was his future. The only way to find out where that path led was to follow.

Making his way down the stairs, he stifled a chuckle at the sound of his brothers' snores. He had almost forgotten the rhythmic sounds of their breathing at night - alternating between the two inhaling and exhaling. He had grown up listening to their nighttime musical interlude - a personal serenade that had the power to lull him to sleep. Neither one would ever admit to making any such noises, but now he had proof.

"What are you doing?" Jessie asked, his voice a raised whisper. He had tuned back into reality in time to see Nadine pour a bottle of rum over top of the treasure chest.

"You know what I'm doing," Nadine replied, striking a match.

"You can't burn that on a ship," Jessie complained. A snort from an adjoining room made him lower his voice before continuing. "You could set the whole place on fire. Some of us aren't proficient swimmers."

"Wait," Nadine said, still holding the lit match. "You don't know how to swim?" She winced as the flame warmed her finger tips before disappearing.

"There are no bodies of water in my home world," Jessie answered through clenched teeth. "We've learnt a few basics, but I'm not sure we are ready to try to swim long distance."

"Huh," Nadine huffed. "Who would have thought?" She struck fire to another match and tossed it on to the chest.

"Aye!" Jessie exclaimed, his knuckles white from clenched fists. He spun in a circle before opening his eyes to a brilliant blue blaze.

"Don't worry," Nadine said. "The magic around the chest will contain the fire. The alcohol should burn off quickly."

"You might have mentioned that before," Jessie complained.

The way the flames danced almost romantically across the top of the chest was alluring. Jessie had seen something similar only once before - necrid flames. They destroyed his home world - a reminder that beauty and safety were not always on the same page. The last of the fire flickered into oblivion, leaving only small chimneys of smoke as proof of its existence. A subtle scent of burnt rum wafted up to his nostrils - his stomach rumbled at the memory of freshly-baked pastries.

"There!" Nadine exclaimed, pointing. Her hand dove deep into the side pocket of her sweater, emerging with a vial.

The cap popped off, sounding more like a bottle of fine champagne opening than the aged blood of a pirate. A drop of thick brownish-red liquid plopped onto a circular burn mark. A grinding noise threatened to wake the others. Neither was sure if it was worry or anticipation that stole both of their breaths away. The lid sprung open, exposing the hidden treasure inside.

"Aha!" Finkle exclaimed. "I knew you two were trying to pull a fast one on me. You didn't think I was going to let you have all the glory, did you?" He pointed a crooked wand at the pirate's chest. "I'll take care of that pearl for now."

"Professor," Jessie started, "you don't understand."

"I don't know what's going on down here," Pandora interrupted, "but if the three of you are done arguing, we have a more pressing matter at hand."

"What is it now?" Finkle asked, inching closer to the treasure.

"Remember the little problem we had on the way back?" Pandora replied. "The one we had to outrun."

"Don't tell me we have a baby squid chasing us," Finkle stated.

"Oh no," Pandora answered.

"Thank goodness."

"We have its mother chasing us!" Pandora yelled.

It took less than a minute to arrange all hands on deck, mouths hanging open at the sight of a passenger ship in the distance being completely destroyed by oversized tentacles.

"We caused that," Dezi blurted out, frowning. "We need to help those people. There must be hundreds on board."

"There is nothing we can do," Finkle stated. "We could barely handle an infant. We'll be destroyed trying to take on a full grown and, I might add, a rather upset one."

"We can't simply leave them!" Pete exclaimed.

"I'm afraid we are going to have to," Danny replied. "Not only are they too far away for us to help, we have other issues to deal with." He pointed to a purple and black sky in the opposite direction. A vivid contrast formed between the course they were heading in and the rising sun everywhere else. Lightning flashed, illuminating a heavy downpour wreaking havoc with the ocean surface.

"Pandora," Finkle yelled, "do something!"

"I'm Goddess of the Sea," Pandora barked back, "not the weather. I suggest everyone hang on."

"That's the best you can do?" Finkle snarled.

"Well, there is one thing we could try." Pandora ran inside and returned with the treasure chest.

"What are you doing?!" Finkle shrieked.

"Giving a child its toy back!" Pandora yelled, over top of growing winds. "It's one thing to make it through that storm; it's another to try and fight a monster at the same time.

Finkle dove, grabbing the pearl. "It can have the chest, but not the contents." He stumbled beneath deck.

Jessie reached out, grabbing Nadine's arm. "Let him go," he said. "At least we know he'll keep it safe for now. We can worry about prying it out of his arms later." He grabbed a knife from inside the chest seconds before Pandora lobbed it into the water.

"Let's hope it was the magic seals on the chest itself that made the little squid happy," Pandora said, the rain whipping against her face in a violent rage.

"If you don't need to be on deck, I suggest you head down!" Danny yelled. "I'll need a couple hands up here to help. This ride is about to get wild." He pointed to what used to be fluffy white clouds, thickening in angry grey tones.

The choppy up and down motion beneath them sent waves thrashing onto the deck. They were sailing into pure anger in liquid form.

Chapter Twenty-Three

"Do we have to steer right into it?" Dezi asked, straining to have his voice heard over the howling wind and crashing waves.

"We don't have a choice," Danny replied. "It's too big to go around. By the time I saw it, we were already being sucked in." His muscles flexed, attempting to hold their course steady - fingers slipping. "This rain is making it hard to keep a grip. If I lose control, be ready to grab the wheel and hold on tight."

"I'm going to strap you in!" Pete yelled. He'd spent an entire summer learning how to properly tie a knot - a practice which, at the time, he had considered useless. Now, he counted his blessings that his father had forced him to learn. Braiding the thick rope around Danny's midsection, he formed the strongest support he could for their young captain.

The rain pelted down. Exposed skin reddened, rubbed raw by the force of the downpour. Pandora stood fast on deck, her hands raised, calming as much of the sea's rage as she could. The path she wove for them was likely the only reason the ship remained in one piece.

"You two better strap in as well!" Danny ordered. "Even with the witch's help, this is going to be a bumpy ride. It's one thing for her to fall over and another for one of us." The boat rocked like a toy model in the swelling sea, almost reaching its tipping point. "Make it fast!"

"On it!" Pete yelled, fitting a coil of rope around Dezi's waist. "I have no desire to be swept away in this." He'd just finished tying off his own rope when a wave lifted their vessel sideways off the surface.

"Hang on!" Danny screamed. "If we make it down, we're going under."

All three grasped the wheel and held on. The wave crashed down beneath them, knocking them sideways. Pandora swung her arms in the opposite direction to their tilt. On her command, the water punched them back into an upright position, but not before thoroughly soaking the deck and lower cabins.

There was no choice but to ignore the screams coming from below. The ocean's temper tantrum wasn't through with them yet. Another massive wave crested before them, leaving nothing else on the horizon.

"Push the engines hard," Danny commanded. "We need to get to the top of this one or it is going to land right on us."

Dezi pushed a lever into high gear. The engines revved. What normally was a loud roar was lost between the boom of thunder and cracks of lightning too close for comfort. The height of the swell grew, gaining momentum as they raced to the top. Making it there was only part of the battle as the boat momentarily sat suspended high above the surface before crashing down again.

"Hang on!" Danny yelled.

The three braced themselves, muscles flexed and teeth grinding in anticipation of impact. Water gushed over top of them, knocking them mercilessly around inside their restraints.

Pete gasped for air in between mouthfuls of salt water. He was drenched head to toe; bruised and battered, but still alive. He glanced at his brother, starting to stir.

Danny groaned. "We shouldn't have made it through that," He admitted, rain still pelting down on his face.

Dezi spat, coughing up some water he had inhaled in the last wave. He glanced up, motioning towards the deck. "Pandora," he muttered. He grabbed his midsection, the presence of pain showing in the grimace making its way onto his face. He gasped, managing to point for a split-second.

Pete's gaze followed his brother's motion towards the body of a woman on her knees, straining to keep the weight of the world on her shoulders. "She's keeping us a float," Pete said. "Let's not waste the opportunity."

Danny was already taking full advantage of the chance. The wheel turned in his grasp. "I think I see a break in the storm up ahead!" he yelled. "Hang on, I'm giving it everything we have left."

With the engines waterlogged and inoperable, the movement of the waves were all they had left to rely on. Turning the wheel at the correct moment launched their vessel towards the break in the storm. A minute later and the ocean calmed. The three boys stood tall. Evidence of nature's viscous attack was merely clouds in the distance.

"We're in the eye," Danny observed, his finger tracing various rainbows in the sky. "Look! There's the island. We made it."

Pete limped over and collapsed beside Pandora. "You okay?" he asked.

Pandora tilted her head in his direction and managed a meek chuckle. "Remind me not to volunteer to help anyone ever again," she muttered.

Jessie poked his head out from the lower level. "Is everyone still here?" he asked. "That was quite the journey."

"We're good," Dezi said, still keeled over. He held a thumb up in the air. "It was a rough ride. How's everyone down there?"

"Banged up," Jessie said. "A couple of helpers from Merliance aren't going to be able to walk for a few days, but we are all alive."

"The Pearl?" Danny asked.

"Don't worry," Jessie replied. "Finkle cushioned it with his own body. He wasn't letting anything happen to it."

"Well, then," Danny said, "let's set anchor. We can assess the injured and figure out who is going ashore. This old girl is going to need repairs if we have any chance making it back." He patted the wheel.

"Over there," Dezi said.

Pointing it out didn't make a difference. A current was already propelling the boat towards a split in the island forming a passageway. The teal water turned dark as they floated into a river. The further they travelled, the denser the plant life became - strangling out the light.

Dezi reached out, his fingertips making contact with some of the low-hanging vegetation. Drops of water from a recent rainfall cascaded down the thick rubbery leaf as it bent under the pressure of his touch. It was only one plant of many making up the vast canopies of dense leaves protecting the area.

"Coming a bit close," Professor Finkle said, limping his way to the wheel. "Are we sure it is deep enough here?"

"Deep enough or not," Danny said, pausing at the sound of a large bird flying unseen overhead, "we don't have a choice. Without engine power, we are at the mercy of the currents." He gazed around, squinting in hopes of catching a glimpse of whatever animal was shrieking undercover of foliage. "Looks like this empties into a lagoon."

The Professor ducked, barely managing to avoid being knocked over by the outstretched wingspan of a large bird. It screeched its dissatisfaction of having missed before disappearing above the tree line again.

"Did that bird try to attack me?" Finkle complained.

"I wouldn't take it personally, Professor," Nadine answered from the stairway. "It was probably trying for the pearl, not you." She nodded at the round white ball tucked under his arm.

"I suppose it is shiny," Finkle commented.

"More than that," Danny interrupted. "If this is a Mermaid Island, you can bet anything that lives here protects that which isn't meant to be touched."

"Yes," Finkle said, rubbing the uneven stubble on his chin. "Well, I have no interest in keeping this trinket. It is merely a key to finding the Fountain of Youth. They can have it back as soon as secrets are revealed."

"Perhaps if you try being a little nicer, people would be more willing to share secrets with you without blackmail," Pandora stated.

"Ah, the Goddess of the Sea," Finkle chuckled. "Flat on your back again, I see. Will you be sitting the rest of this adventure out?"

"I might like to follow along," Pandora snarled back. "It might be interesting to see how all of this plays out."

"I don't know why you bothered to come at all," Finkle complained. "You've been rather useless, if you ask me."

Pandora pulled herself to a sitting position. "What was that?"

"Take a look around!" Finkle exclaimed. "The boat is a mess and people are injured. Your job was a simple one - to get us here in one piece. I'd grade your performance with a failing mark."

"To be honest," Danny said, "without Pandora, none of us would be here. We should have been torn in two. You should be thanking the stars we are in as good a shape as we are."

"Someone best be working on a way home," Finkle huffed. He walked over and nudged Pandora with his shoe. "It looks to me as if this Sea Goddess is all washed up." He turned to the brothers. "Now that's a proper pun." He laughed.

"I wouldn't count her out," Jessie replied.

"I would," Finkle answered. "Look at her. All her power is spent." He leaned over top of her face and flashed a crooked smile. "Even the horsemen in her box of surprises aren't speaking to her." He straightened up - back cracking. "We can all learn an important lesson from her, though."

"And what's that?" Pandora scoffed.

"Simple," Finkle explained. "Don't use all your gas before you cross the finish line." He pulled out his wand.

"I thought you said you were a potion master," Pete said.

"I am," Finkle said. "I'm also quite efficient with a wand..."

"We're as far as we are going to go," Danny announced. "We are at a standstill. I'm not even sure we need an anchor."

"Drop it anyways," Finkle ordered. He pulled a tab on an orange raft, waiting several minutes for it to expand before taking a seat inside. "Those of you coming ashore, let's go. The rest of you - hoist this baby down."

Pete glanced around, looking for the source of a barely audible noise. "What is that?" he asked. "It sounds like children giggling."

"That," Pandora whispered back, smiling, "is a good friend of mine. Someone you might know as Karma. The Professor is in a world of trouble now. Do me a favour and don't tell him. I want to be there to see the look on his face."

Chapter Twenty-Four

Finkle dropped to his knees and kissed the sandy beach. "Finally, dry land!" he hollered. "I think I detest water even more than I did before."

Nadine made a circle. "It's beautiful!" Rays of sunlight poked holes in white fluffy clouds, glistening down softly before becoming shimmers in the clear water. Nothing was left to the imagination. Multi-coloured fish swam below the surface, hovering above white sands. This was the place dreams were made of. "Perfectly untouched by man."

"Ahem," the Professor coughed. "While I'd love to agree..." He used a finger to make poking motions in the air.

Nadine's eye's followed the motion. She gasped. "A raft?!" she shrieked. "How would that be here?"

"Looks well-built," Danny said, walking over. He had hung back from the others, keeping an eye on the unfolding events. It wasn't the best situation. Technically, he only had Nadine to rely on and Jessie - whose trust wasn't yet earned. The rest of his team was still on board, making repairs or injured. It was little consolation that Pete and Dezi had remained behind to help as well. "Whoever did this has some survival skills."

"I built it," a tanned figure called out, spear in hand. "Now, why don't you explain who you are and what you are doing here?"

"You can start with why you have that egg," a woman added, moving beside him.

"We came to return it," Nadine offered, cupping a hand over her eyes. The strangers had picked the perfect spot to appear. The sun going down behind them made it impossible to see who they were talking to, or how many others could be with them.

"Where did you find it?" the woman snarled. "And how did you know to bring it here?"

"It was hidden in a pirate treasure," Nadine explained.

"Egg?" Finkle muttered, one eyebrow arched. He chuckled to himself - this treasure was more valuable than he anticipated. That knowledge alone put him one step closer to eternal youth. "Is this not the Mermaid sanctuary?!" he yelled out, gasping afterwards, his breath strangled by the humidity. He reached for a handkerchief, but stopped mid-motion, realizing it would be futile to attempt to control sweat. The drops cascading down his face merely added to his already-soaked attire.

"How did you know that?!" the woman shrieked.

"Because," Danny explained, "we are from Merliance."

"Thank goodness," the man replied. "I'm getting too old to worry about thieves and bandits." He loosened his grip on the spear.

"Are you..." Nadine stuttered. The information processing in her mind mixed with emotions. She had heard about them all her life, but never imagined one day she would be face to face with them.

"Are we what?" the woman asked, tilting her head for a better view of the girl.

"I think you might be my great-grandmother," Nadine answered. Her legs buckled beneath her.

Chapter Twenty-Five

The family gathering ended up short-lived. After the initial shock wore off, there was the moment of disbelief - searching for visible evidence of their relation. Acceptance had come in the form of a group hug - which was about all they had time for.

They discussed the most prominent family moments as the crude raft carried them down a side river to a hidden pool. In the centre, a spiral rock formation acted as an incubator for a few dozen eggs - one spot noticeably empty.

"Quickly now," Viola said. "Replace the egg."

Finkle planted his feet on solid ground again. He sighed scratching his head with the tip of his wand. "I'm afraid I can't do that."

"Can't do that?!" Viola echoed. "I thought you were here to return it. You've tricked us." Her voice became cold and rough.

"Oh no," Finkle said, waving his wand in the air. "Don't get all riled up. I have every intention of returning this egg, I simply want something in return."

"Professor..." Jessie started.

"Not now, good boy," Finkle said. "I'm negotiating. You should have listened to me when I said women were nothing but trouble." He pointed the wand at Nadine's temple. "Then you wouldn't care what happens to her."

"What is it you want?" Viola asked.

"I want to speak with a Mermaid," Finkle answered. "I want to know the location of the Fountain of Youth."

"That's a myth," George complained. "You won't find it here. We've lived here a very long time. We would have found it by now if it existed."

"Unfortunately, my good man," Finkle said, applying enough pressure on his wand to create an indent in Nadine's skin, "you are most definitely not a Mermaid." He glanced over his shoulder, a splash stealing his attention.

"I'm telling you, there is no Fountain of Youth," Viola argued. "You, sir, are playing a dangerous game."

"Dangerous?" Finkle said, spitting out the side of his mouth. "I don't see it that way. I am a Good Samaritan returning this egg to its mother. I think one good deed deserves another, don't you?"

"Professor," Jessie started.

"Ah," Finkle interrupted. "Don't even try it. I've had my fill of the lot of you. When we started out, I was sure we had a common purpose. How quickly you forgot your sister and how this discovery can save her."

"I haven't forgotten her," Jessie snapped back. "I just feel there has to be a better way. You are holding a child."

"Yes," Finkle said. "I am and the life of the young lady you hold such interest in as well. That puts me in charge."

Jessie gasped. The helplessness he felt acted like lead in his shoes, pinning him to the spot. His eyes watered, watching red flush into Nadine's cheeks at the mention of his feelings - feelings that seemed to strengthen by the second. "Please," he begged. "Let her go."

"You aren't in any position to ask favours," Finkle answered. "I want to see a Mermaid. I know they are here, splashing about."

Viola sighed, her eyes shut tight. "You are making a mistake. Mermaids have allowed us to live in this world relatively unaffected by their will. They are a peaceful and powerful race who, for the most part, keep to themselves. Their numbers, however, are dwindling. Fewer eggs have been making it to maturity. Each one is a chance to replenish their numbers. Don't steal that from them. Give them a reason to renew their faith in land dwellers."

A fish tail flopped out of the pool, smacking back down - the water rippling from the movement.

"There she is," Finkle cooed.

"There who is?" Pandora asked, appearing on the other side of the pool the echo of children's laughter in the distance accompanying her.

"Pandora!" Finkle scoffed.

"Did you miss me?"

"If you are here to try to stop me..." the Professor started, tightening his grip on his wand.

"I'm a mere spectator," Pandora said. "I have no intentions of lifting a finger to intervene in whatever happens."

"Good," Finkle answered, his eyes glued to the woman, unable to trust her words. "Now, back to my Mermaid meeting."

A Mermaid's head broke through the surface of the water, her long teal hair noticeable dry. Her lips parted, revealing an array of dancing colours. She closed it again without uttering a noise.

"I have something that belongs to you," Finkle teased.

The Mermaid opened her mouth again, her words forming a melody carried on the rays of a rainbow. "I know what you seek. I have been listening." She submerged, disappearing. The clear water showed every detail below - every detail except the Mermaid's whereabouts. She reappeared in front of Jessie, this time showing more of her torso.

Jessie gasped at the sight unfolding before him. The woman's long teal hair blew freely in the wind. Prismatic scales formed iridescent armour plating, casting rainbows when light gently kissed their surface. The range of colours extended far beyond that which he had previously known.

"I want to know what you want," she sang. "Do you search for the Fountain of Youth? What price would you pay to find it?"

"Does it exist?" Jessie muttered, unable to break his stare.

"What is it you seek the answer to time for?"

"My sister," Jessie whispered. "It would save her from certain death. I would do anything for her." He felt himself begin to sway, yet he was unable to move - even the formation of words took effort. For the first time in his life he felt weak.

"You say you would do anything," the Mermaid said. "Would you kill for it?"

Jessie gasped, unsure about his answer. He opened his mouth but no words formed, his mind still contemplating the question. Could he kill to save his sister?

"You must decide that answer," the Mermaid continued. "There is only one way to the Fountain of Youth. You have the means in your pocket."

Jessie's hand plunged inside, having forgotten about the blade he had retrieved from the chest before it went overboard. He felt it slice his skin before pulling it out. "The only way to find the liquid of time," he muttered, his gaze now locked on the reflection of scales on the surface of the blade. He shook, understanding what would have to be done. "You are the Fountain of Youth," he mumbled.

Although the knife had been locked away, it hadn't escaped the test of time completely. The handle found its way into Jessie's grip, warped and crooked. The blade had sat idle far too long. Now it longed for the taste of flesh, calling out to its handler to use all of its powers.

"Yes," the Mermaid answered. "Through my veins runs the very thing you seek. Only that blade can penetrate my scales to retrieve it. You have the power to save your sister in your hands."

Jessie pushed one foot forward. His body shook. How does one choose between saving someone they love and murder? He fell to his knees, the knife tumbling out of his hand onto the sand. "I can't," he admitted. "My sister gave her life essence to save others. She could never live knowing a life was taken in exchange for hers."

"Perhaps you can't!" Finkle yelled, lunging forward. His hand grasped the blade. "But I can."

The Professor launched the egg in the air, causing Danny to jump to catch it and avoiding further interference from Merliance's finest. Finkle smiled at his handy work, seeing the boy land hard on his back, the wind knocked out of him.

"Professor," Pandora said.

"Don't waste your time, woman," Finkle replied. "I haven't used any of my energy and you don't have any left. This is a good time to learn silence."

Pandora shrugged her shoulders. "Have it your way." She crossed her arms over her chest.

Nadine gasped. With her great-grandparents busying themselves returning the egg; Danny showing no signs of moving; Pandora keeping to herself; and Jessie emotionally spent, there was no one left to stop the Professor. She could still feel the imprint of magic from his wand on her temple - it was stronger than anything she had in her arsenal. A tear streaked down her face as she alternated glances between the Mermaid and the Professor. A shadow caught her attention and her breath. She stumbled backwards, landing on the sand. She felt a sharp pain in her hand, followed by a warmth she knew was blood. She had fallen on a stray piece of driftwood.

Finkle laughed. "Is that the best Merliance has to offer? I'll be taking that drink now," he said, moving one foot forward. His smile mutated into a grimace as he felt a squeezing sensation in his midsection. He looked down at a large tentacle pinning both hands and their contents against his chest. "Pandora, do something!" he yelled with all the breath he could muster.

"I'm just a spectator, Professor," Pandora replied, examining her manicure. "If you hadn't told me to be quiet, I might have been able to tell you Karma had come for you, bringing mama squid along for the ride. I found them in the lagoon looking for something. I think we can safely say, it is the magic on that blade they are attracted to."

Finkle's eyes widened, as the tentacle lifted high in the air, before splashing back down and disappearing.

"He did want to be here for the big finish," Pandora joked, laughing at herself. "Everyone else okay?" she asked.

"I think so," Danny squeaked, holding his thumb upright in the air.

"You have returned my child," the Mermaid said, "and renewed my faith in your kind. Now go. The act of replacing the missing egg has started a magical reaction to move this island to a safer location. You will need to be out of the area before that happens."

"That's our cue," Pandora said, helping Danny to his feet. She took as much of his weight as she could, hobbling back to the raft.

"This is our stop," Viola declared as they approached the lagoon.

"You're not coming back with us?!" Nadine shrieked. "I've just found you. I won't lose you again."

Viola rubbed her shoulders. "We've been here too long to live any other way." She glanced at her husband. "This is where we want to spend out our time. This is our home."

Tears formed in the corners of Nadine's eyes, "But..."

"But nothing," Viola said. "This is what is right for us. You have to follow what is right for you." She nodded at Jessie. "He's a fine young man. Follow your heart." Her lips brushed against Nadine's forehead. "Now hurry, before you are stuck here with us."

Nadine froze, watching her great-grandparents hand-in-hand jump from the raft to the sand. The white noise of splashing water filled her ears, unable to differentiate between the paddle hitting the water's surface and the sound of her own tears.

"Nadine," Jessie called, extending his hand. "You need to climb."

They were already back at the boat. Nadine glanced over her shoulder at the shore one last time. A dense fog had swooped in, erasing sight of everything. There was no sign left of her family - the way they wanted it.

"Are you two coming?!" Dezi yelled over the sound of a revving engine. "We are back in business and ready to shove off."

Nadine took Jessie's hand. "Yeah," she answered. "Don't worry about us."

Chapter Twenty-Six

"Welcome back," Lawrence said.

"Thank you," Jessie answered. After all they had been through, he found himself back where he began - in front of the Overseers.

"We've read the reports and want to say, well done," Lawrence stated. "You proved your worthiness to our organization."

"Sir," Jessie said, widening his stance, his hands locked together behind his back. "My brothers."

Lawrence waved one hand in the air, his head shaking. "No worries," he replied. "We have no intentions of detaining them."

"Thank you," Jessie said.

"I suppose they will be continuing a search for a cure for your sister?" Lawrence asked. "Do they have any other leads?"

"Nothing concrete," Jessie answered. "But they will find something. I have given you my word, and as such, I will be remaining here."

"Yes," Lawrence said, "You are a member of Merliance now. That doesn't mean you will be here, though."

"What?" Nadine blurted out.

"Don't play dumb, dear," Veronica said. "It doesn't suit a girl of your intelligence. Obviously we have members outside these walls."

"But," Nadine complained. "I know everyone."

"Are you telling me you have never noticed anyone disappear?" Veronica asked. "I'm sure you can think of at least one."

"Abigail," Nadine whispered, emotions balling up in her stomach.

"Which brings us to an interesting coincidence," Lawrence said. "A while back, there was a big uproar over the unearthing of some remains by an archeological team."

"Archaeology was Abigail's favourite subject," Nadine mumbled.

"Indeed," Lawrence agreed. "She was the best we had in that department. When rumours began flying that the remains were proof Mermaids existed, we sent her to investigate."

"She's alive?!" Nadine cried.

"Well, of course she is alive," Veronica answered. "She altered a bit of evidence to put enough doubt in the findings. We were lucky to scrape by with our secret intact."

"Afterwards," Lawrence continued, "she remained on as part of the team, in case the need arises again. She sends reports in every so often. It is the last communication we received that is of particular interest."

"Why is that?" Nadine asked.

"It seems they are looking for an artifact of interest," Veronica replied. "They have found a trail that leads to the fabled Holy Grail."

"The Holy Grail?" Jessie repeated, his eyes widening. "It is said to grant eternal youth to anyone who drinks from it."

"Or eternal life," Lawrence agreed. "Regardless, this whole ordeal had us considering the possibility that we should be investigating such claims... purely for research."

"We are assigning you two to the job," Veronica advised.

"Since your brothers are going the same way," Lawrence added, "we see no reason why you shouldn't work together."

"Why are you doing this?" Jessie asked.

Lawrence sighed. "We needed to know where you stood on the morality scale. You proved your integrity and loyalty - bottom line, we trust you."

"And me?" Nadine squeaked.

Veronica smiled. "We all have a path to follow. Sometimes that route takes us outside where we thought we would be. We have all taken this under consideration and it is a unanimous decision that you belong on this quest."

Nadine nodded. Leaving the only home she had ever known wouldn't be easy, but deep in her heart, she knew the Overseers were right. This was what she was meant to do, just as her great-grandparents were meant to remain on the Island. "When do we start?" she asked.

"As soon as the repairs are made to the boat," Lawrence stated. "Consider it a going-away gift from all of us. We expect to receive updates and reports on a regular basis still. Both of you remain an important part of Merliance."

"I object!" Pandora shrieked, dragging four guards behind her.

"You object to us releasing these two on their own accordance?" Lawrence asked, one eyebrow arching.

"Yes!" Pandora cried. "I... wait, did you say you are setting them free?"

"Indeed," Lawrence replied. "Unless you believe we should keep them here with us. We are willing to listen to all arguments."

"No," Pandora said, shaking the guards to the floor. "I'll just be on my way." She pointed over her shoulder. Her fingers snapped as she walked backwards towards the exit.

"We'll meet you at the boat," Nadine said.

"The boat," Pandora mouthed.

"The Overseers are giving it to us so we can continue our quest," Jessie explained. "It's getting a few repairs done before we leave."

Nadine took Jessie's hand, taking a moment to enjoy the warmth that came with the tiniest squeeze. She wasn't sure how she felt about seeing Abigail again, but she was certain it wouldn't affect the way she felt about the person standing beside her.

"Do we know which way we are headed?" Nadine asked.

"You'll find maps and notes on board," Lawrence explained. "We are also loading up enough supplies to last you a while."

"Remember," Veronica added, "we are family. If you need anything, we are here to help. Don't be afraid to ask."

Pandora waited until the three were outside to speak again. "What is that?"

"A memento," Nadine answered. "Before this journey began, I was having mixed emotions about not having anything to remember Viola and George by. When I fell on the beach, I landed on this. I think it's from the original boat they took to return the stolen eggs. It might seem silly, it is merely an old piece of drift wood, but I'm glad I brought it back."

A single ray from the sun broke through dense white clouds, illuminating a simple plank of wood made beautiful by the effects of time. An artist known as the ocean hand carved it, hiding stories of adventures past within smooth grooves.

"I don't think it's silly," Jessie commented. "In some cases, time can do beautiful things. I hope you realize we aren't looking to change what should naturally happen. I only want to return that which was stolen from my sister. She deserves a chance to become as beautiful as that piece of wood in her own time."

"If you two are finished being all mushy," Pandora interrupted, "perhaps someone could tell me where are we going? Do we have a new plan?"

"We do," Jessie replied. "We about to embark on a quest for the Holy Grail. This time, I know we'll find a way to save Victoria."

"I think you might be right," Nadine replied. "There's no way we could fail with the team we have."

"Hey," Danny called out. "Wait up. I'm coming along for the ride." He fired off a wink that even found Pandora blushing.

"Why do I have a feeling the world isn't ready for us?" Nadine asked.

"They better be!" Danny exclaimed. "Like it or not, we're on our way! Next stop: the Holy Grail."

Author's Message

I hope you enjoyed reading *Finding the Fountain of Youth* as much as I did writing it. Watch for new books in this series in 2018, including:

The Quest for the Holy Grail

&

The Hunt for the Cinamani Stone

Other Titles from C.A. King

Shattering the Effects of Time

Join the Shinning brothers, Jessie, Dezi and Pete as they set out on a quest to save their younger sister. No magic known to them or their friends has ever been able to reverse the grip of time. A few legends, however, exist mentioning ancient items that may hold the key to do exactly that.

This brand new series will take you on a search for the Fountain of Youth and Mermaids; a quest for the Holy Grail; a trip to visit Daryl the mountain guru, in the hunt for the Cinamani Stone; on a search for Ambrosia, the food of the Gods; and other adventures.

When Leaves Fall: A Different Point of View Story

Ralph wakes up to what others only experience in a nightmare. Chained to a shed, he has no idea where he is, or who his captor is. His memories a blurred at best. As the days press on he finds himself experiencing a roller coaster of feelings. Hunger, thirst and pain become his only companions. Flashbacks of a happier time are all he has to keep him going. As his situation deteriorates, he finds himself doubting the very things he wants most - a family.

When Leaves Fall is a dramatic-thriller with a twist. Keep the tissue box close for the ending.

Tomoiya's Story

A Vampire Tale. She had a secret but she wasn't the only one who had something to hide.

Book I ~ Escape to Darkness

Book II ~ Collection Tears

Book III~ Coming Soon

Peach Coloured Daisies: A Cursed by the Gods Story

He couldn't die. An ancient curse meant she always did. This time, that was going to change - one way or another.

When Daisy's grandmother, her last living relative, passes away, she doesn't know where to turn. Things go from bad to worse when a local psychic tells her about a curse. Alone and confused, she ends up in front of her college professor's office, ready to cry her heart out in his arms.

Matt Demi might be the son of a God, but he's living the life of a cursed man. He's had to watch the woman he loves die on her twenty-first birthday countless times. Nothing he does seems to be able to affect the outcome. When she shows up at his office scared out of her wits by a psychic's prediction, he vows this time will be different.

With only three days, Matt will need to embrace a side of him he swore off long ago to save her, but will he lose himself in the process?

Flower Shields: A Four Horsemen Novel

Meet the four horsemen: Michael, Gabrielle, Uriel and Raphael. For centuries their job has been to guard the gates of hell, making sure they never open. Without the keys, there was never any real threat. That's about to change. There are rumours on the horizon that demon followers unearthed scrolls that explain exactly how to find the lost keys. This new battle is a race to see which side locates them first.

Michael couldn't care less about the love story behind how and why the world was created. In fact, nothing matters to him other than keeping the gates to hell closed. If one of the lost keys ever fell into the wrong hands, all humanity would be doomed. He's not going to let that happen - at any cost.

****

Tara's life is nothing short of a disaster. She's managed to flunk out of college with about the same amount of dignity as every relationship she's been in. The only constant in her life has been her love for flowers. When she's attacked at work, a stranger comes to her aid. Michael might be good-looking, but he's also arrogant, bossy and crazy. He's also her only chance to figure out who attacked her and why. Should she follow her heart and trust him - or listen to her head and run?

The Portal Prophecies

These great titles in C.A. King's The Portal Prophecies series are available now at most online book retailers:

A Keeper's Destiny

A Halloween's Curse

Frost Bitten

Sleeping Sands

Deadly Perceptions

Finding Balance

The prophecies are the key to their survival. Can they solve them in time?

Surviving the Sins: Answering the Call

The prophecies are being rewritten. This time someone is using the seven deadly sins: Lust; Gluttony; Greed; Sloth; Wrath; Envy; and Pride, to unlock an ancient evil. The book falls into Jade's hands to answer destiny's call. Can she survive the sins?

Surviving the Sins: Pride

No one is safe when a witch's pride is at stake.

Prudance is back in Pewterclaw, and she isn't about to give up her prestigious status without a fight - especially not because of vampires. As an eighth-generation witch, she plans to do whatever it takes to stop the proposed new legislation from becoming law, including waking the dead for help.

Humility isn't in her vocabulary. With an ego spinning out of control and ancestral power at her fingertips, Prudance weaves a plot to keep Jade and Gavin separated. Will it be enough to satisfy the spirits she summoned?

When her pride costs more than she bargained for, someone has to pay the tab - but who will it be?

www.ingramcontent.com/pod-product-compliance
Lightning Source LLC
Chambersburg PA
CBHW031113260626
47172CB00001B/339